The Mark of Betrayal

Ember Blackwell

Contents

1. Chapter 1 1

2. Chapter 2 9

3. Chapter 3 11

4. Chapter 4 16

5. Chapter 5 22

6. Chapter 6 27

7. Chapter 7 31

8. Chapter 8 36

9. Chapter 9 41

10. Chapter 10 44

11. Chapter 11 48

12. Chapter 12 54

13. Chapter 13 58

14. Chapter 14 62

15. Chapter 15 67

16. Chapter 16   73

17. Chapter 17   78

18. Chapter 18   82

19. Chapter 19   88

20. Chapter 20   94

21. Chapter 21   99

22. Chapter 22   104

23. Chapter 23   111

24. Chapter 24   117

25. Chapter 25   122

26. Chapter 26   130

27. Chapter 27   137

28. Chapter 28   143

29. Chapter 29   150

30. Chapter 30   155

31. Chapter 31   160

32. Chapter 32   166

33. Chapter 33   173

34. Chapter 34   179

35. Chapter 35   185

36. Chapter 36   190

37. Chapter 37   196

38. Chapter 38   209

39. Chapter 39   217

40. Chapter 40   227

41. Epilogue   235

Chapter 1

C iane

I groan and hit my alarm off with my werewolf strength trying to ignore the chores that I know await me. My eyes hardly coordinate with my entire body, begging me to go back to sleep and avoid the cold that was currently grasping onto me like a leech.

However, even I knew I couldn't do that. With little will power and determination, I pluck the duvet and rush to the bathroom.

I glare at my reflection on the cracked mirror and almost feel disappointed with what I see. I was rather slim with my shoulder length brown hair and mud brown eyes. My upper lip is thinner than my lower and a small birth mark laid on the base of my nose. The most prominent feature being the pink thick scar that runs along the side of my face, fully showing the intentions of the culprit who left it there.

It disgusts me.

I abruptly look away and strip, taking a much needed shower from all the previous chores and activities.

I had stayed up late last night, busy preparing the meals. I never get a day off like most people do. I slave and work in the kitchen with the omegas of the pack. It wasn't always this bad. It wasn't always this painful yet, I had to adapt to it or be trampled on, be beaten or work. Each time I chose the latter.

My parents, I recall, were the best and when they were with me, I didn't have to work so hard. It has been too many years since they died and the memories we shared never faded. How they cared, loved and took care of me so gently. I was so young but those were the best days of my life. None I've ever had ever again.

Shutting off the rather depressing thoughts is quite hard but necessary. The consequences of not doing so still laying too vividly in my mind.

Each morning, I am required to wake up early and work with the rest of the omegas. I became one by default. Who would want to accept an orphan, really with no family members and zero friends.

I sigh when I find the kitchen empty. The omegas find joy in letting me suffer for they know I'll always be at the receiving end of any punishment given. It's what I've known. I loath it, hate it yet, I let the feeling remain.

Picking everything I need to make breakfast, I begin making pancakes so that maybe they can join me when I'm done or when I'm nearly done.

The alpha hated me even more for reasons I had never comprehended and I am always the one to pay and receive more punches or slaps than the rest. He had instilled pure fear within me and he knew this. He finds bliss in my cower, in the tears that trail down my frail form and cheeks. He finds ecstasy in the pain that I endure at his hands. He loves the pain I feel and I have seen genuine smiles form on his lips. I have witnessed how psychotic he really is.

He finds pleasure in my pain, a type of pain, I would not wish on anyone.

They didn't show for about an hour and that hour depletes my strength. When they did, I could see the smug looks being shot my way and I instantly realize their intentions.

My eyes find the loving couples displaying affection as I served their breakfast. I stare at the loving mates all cuddled up, feeding and being cute to each other. Their soulmate. The one made for them.

Mate.

A word every wolf desires and wants to hear. My parents were mates and they loved each other so much. They made me believe it too, even believe that everyone is good somehow. I used to believe it, live even by it, but as time went by I realized that people lie and enjoy other people's suffering so why would I tolerate them and think they are good.

I have never desired mates, but if I were to encounter him, I wanted them to be from a different pack. Not one that has found peace in my tears.

My mind lights up when I realize that tomorrow is my birthday. The day I'm supposed to find my mate, the other half of my soul, or so they say.

I let out a long groan as I try to rest my already hurting body. I walk to the tiny closet and ramage through it, pull out a tattered old book, the cover that once was ivory white, now an earth brown with tears on almost every page.

I've always loved reading because it usually teleports me from my harsh reality to a much better place, a place I wish I was. It makes me feel emotions that the characters are feeling and that's what's capture my heart. It makes me temporarily forget how terrible my life really is.

I don't know for how long I read but I'm interrupted by the sudden slamming open of my door. I glance up from my book, still slightly emersed in the world or my character.

My face instantly pales when my eyes meet the man. I stare at him expectantly and he walks towards me, almost losing his footing. His eyes look too red and I could smell the liquor on him and I realize he's drunk.

"A...alpha?" I question, fear flowing through every vein in my body.

He stumbles towards me and I quickly shoot out of bed, backing away towards my tiny closet. He walks towards me until he's right in front of me. An instant pain shoot through my face and my face snaps to the side.

He slapped me.

"D... don't you dare look me in the eye, you trash!" He slurs and gives me another slap to my cheek and it hurts. I could feel the sting of tears in my eyes.

He keeps going at it, hitting and slapping me enjoying my whimpers and groans of pain. Before my mind can register, he begins unbuckling his pants and my eyes widen in pure horror and complete terror.

"Wh..what are y...you doing Alpha?" I stutter, my face burning from all the hits and slaps.

"Shut up, you slut!" He snaps before turning my face and pressing his disgusting lips on mine. He grabs my shoulder in a tight grasp, pulling my frail body towards my tiny bed.

Tears flood my eyes almost instantly and in pain. He can beat me, hit me, slap me, hell he can even cut me but I won't let myself be used sexually. I won't let him do that for it's the only thing that is keeping my dignity and me from shattering.

Mustering all the strength in me, I shove him off before hitting him hard on his crotch. This makes his hold on me loosen and I immediately race out of my room, tears cascading down my face in pain and utter misery.

I knew he hated me but to try and rape me is beyond the things that I thought he'd try to do to me. Tears keeps running down my cheeks as I recall everything he just did to me. I rub my lips harshly against my sweater that they begin to hurt as I try to get the image if his lips on mine for my head. This doesn't work as tears keeps streaming.

I suddenly collapse down on the damp grass near the pack border. I'm wise enough not to cross the it. Pulling my knees to my chest, and an uncontrolled sob escapes my lips as I recall everything that has gone wrong in my life. For my dead parents, for the pain I've had to endure, for all the things I've gone through. My eyes begin to droop from crying so much and I even don't try to stop it or resist it as my vision get blurry and the world turns dark.

When I come to, it was still dark and that actually made me glad. It would make my escape even more easier. All this time I've been holding on, trying not to break even when I was being hated and beaten, and abused. I've been trying to keep myself together hoping that maybe my life would get better but today made me realize that nothing will get better. In fact, things will get worst for me and I will end up losing even my will to live which has happened more than once.

If the alpha wanted to rape me, what would prevent all those other guys from not doing the same? What would stop them from taking everything away from me?

Getting up from the cold grass, I crawl back to the pack house to get the few things that I call my own. It only took ten minutes for me to get to the pack house and I immediately head to my poorly lit room. Grabbing a small tattered duffle bag bought by my parents years ago, I stuff the few clothes in before heading to the kitchen. I grab a few loaves of bread and bottles of water and placing them in my bag.

An amazing sweet scent wafts itself to my nose and I immediately sniff the air. I turn ready to make my final escape but my step halts as a sharp pain shoots through my shoulder. I glance at it and stare at a silver knife sticking out of it.

My brown eyes snaps up and they meet with the green ones of the alpha and immediately my world comes crushing down as we both utter one word that I was never cared for and hating it right now.

"Mate."

No. My fate can't be that cruel. The goddess can't curse me this way. After all I've gone through, after all the pain I've been through?! Don't I deserve some form of peace or a sweet mate?

"Oh goddess. This is impossible." He whispers, his eyes trained on me and for the first time in my life, I'm staring at warm green eyes that if I didn't know him well I would have thought he was a nice guy. A worthy mate, a mate worth fighting and waiting for.

Grabbing the knife on my shoulder, I pull it out as whimpers of pain leave my lips. He stares at my shoulder, in both pain and horror. He caused this.

Through his distraction, I turn towards the door before sprinting away with the little amount of strength that I had left in me. I could hear footsteps behind me but I don't turn to check who it is.

"Please stop!" I hear the alpha scream as his footsteps get closer to me which only made me push myself even harder. I could see the border already and I couldn't wait to cross it. Passing the dazed border patrol, I cross over breathing heavily knowing he can't cross it himself.

"Please stop! I'm so sorry." He whispers, his voice cracking in the process and that makes me scoff.

"What do you want?" I glare at him with all the hate that I could muster and feeling the urge to destroy him, to make him feel all the pain I've gone through, the torture I've endured at his pathetic hands.

"Please come back. I'm so sorry." He whispers, emotions.spilling thought those words, I could see tears brimming in his eyes. If someone would have told me a few days ago that the cruel alpha would be shedding tears because for me, I would have laughed so hard and called them psycho.

"So you can finally rape me? Or chain me to the wall as you punish me for something I totally have no clue about?" I spat my venom filled words and I see him flinch.

"Just tell me your name, please." He begs in utter misery and I let out a humorless chuckle. Of course he doesn't know my name. I've been called all those cliche names and I'm tired. Tired of enduring, tired of the pain. Tired, angry and emotionally drained but most importantly, I'm beyond mad.

I'm mad for all those things they've done to me. I'm angry at everything and everyone. I'm so freaking angry and I swear that the next time he sees me, he'll regret every pain he has inflicted on me, the crude words, the pain filled words, everything he has done.

With that, I offer him a response. A promise of pain, a promise of vengeance before turning and speeding away into the still, cold and ominous night.

"I'm your worst nightmare."

Chapter 2

I run with everything I've got in me knowing that stopping will only show how weak I have been all my life. I have let him walk all over me. I have let him hurt me emotionally, physically and mentally.

Everyone has found pleasure in the tears in my eyes and the pain in my heart.

All those years I've suffered in that pack. All the time I cried myself to sleep at night wondering what tomorrow was going to offer. If I'm going to live or die by being tortured.

No, I'm not running to another pack. I better go to a human town or something like that. Packs are overrated. People think and believe that pack life is about living happily, having pups with their mates and having happy ever afters.

They know nothing about suffering, about discrimination, about being judged, about being different.

I didn't know that once my parents die, I was going to be a slave to my pack. A place where I had lived all my life and known for happiness.

I continue running to nowhere in particular as I thank the goddess for the small ward if cash I had. People overrate packs but I will show them that packs are about suffering and pain.

Packs destroys our lives while those with ranks are respected. Lower ranked wolves are humiliated and tortured and made to feel so inferior.

I swear the next time they see me, they'll regret ever hating me, ever speaking badly to me. They'll regret each and every pain for the last nine years.

Some may say those are just few years but if you were me you'd understand, because it's only me that can understand the pain I went through there.

The choices I make now will be my own. They will never be based off my por excuse of a mate or anyone else for that matter. I will make each and everyone of them regret it. This is not a threat, this is a promise, a promise of the oncoming revenge.

Why make mere threats that I'm not going to do anything. They overrate packs. But they under estimated me and that's their first slip up but my first lesson.

A lesson for life.

Chapter 3

I don't know how long I ran but when I stopped my strength was already depleted and I fell down. A heavy sigh came rushing out of my lips as I laid on the dump grass, my chest heaving as the memories of my life came rushing back. How I have been pushed and tossed. How I've been humiliated and rejected by everyone. No wonder some people commit suicide.

Without support one tends to crumble. Even though humans don't believe it, we need each other in survive. We need love to survive, it's that family love that pushes us to our limits, love for your mate,your daughter that makes everything worth it.

Without any of that the struggle we make are not worth it. It's that love that makes us stronger and when it doesn't exist, we break for it's through people that we survive. It's through those people again that we die and get destroyed.

I lay down feeling my strength coming back a little bit. I stand up on shaky legs as I grab a nearby tree to support my weak limbs. I pull out the piece of bread I had packed and munch on it peacefully, as peaceful as my tormented brain can get.

I eat about four slices before stuffing the rest into my duffle bag and grabbing some water. I gulp the entire bottle down and rest my head on the tree.

I flop down on the dirty forest floor feeling my energy drained even more as my vision as my vision fades. Before I can resist it, I slip into unconsciousness.

I woke up with a jolt, looking around noticing how dark it already is. I must have slept for hours. I stretch feeling alot more stronger than before.

I grab my bag standing up and walking away with no semse of direction at all. My feet hurts so much and even though I'm alot stronger than before, I feel so sore after running for the many hours.

I start walking even though my body is protesting, begging me to still rest even though I know I'm stronger than before,heck stronger than when I was at the pack.

Everything is dead quiet and I keep turning around. I am beyond scared. I had never gone out before in my pack and being out here makes all my fears surface, after all darkness is the place of demons.

I inhale deeply trying to erase all the bad memories from my past, even though its permanently stuck with me, scarred to my brain that wherever I'd go the pain that is in my heart would always be there and that I'd never fully heal no matter what.

I'd lie and say its okay but it's definitely not okay. It hurts so much but I just gotta be strong, for revenge. Most people leave their packs and come back as badasses or smoking hot.

I don't want any of that. I don't want my ex mate to be jealous, I just want him to feel pain, the same pain I've felt for years, the pain that I went through each ands every one ght lulling myself to sleep since it was at night that my inner torment always began.

I grabbed a few vines as I walked, just walking aimlessly with no sense of direction. I'm used to pain and this is nothing to the things I've endured.

I keep stumbling over roots and other hidden things on the cold soil. My shoes are so much tattered that I can feel the cold grass and mud on my feet.

Suddenly a gigantic growl resonate through my left making fear crawl through every nerve of my body and without warning, I begin shaking like a frail leaf. This is what I was afraid of, rogues who have lost their minds. This always happen in every story, in every movie.

I turn around just in time to see a gigantic wolf leaping through the air trying to grab my neck. I side step and it rams itself to a nearby tree.

I take steps back staring at the gigantic animal before me with it's bright red eyes. I gulp fearfully as it approaches me slowly taunting me. I know it can smell my fear, it knows I'm scared.

Its red eyes glowing mischievously and evilly making me gulp once again as I stare intently into to see its next move.

It growls loudly walking towards me as I took steps back tears already forming in my eyes.

How am I going to defend myself, considering how clueless I am. I know that sometimes before I had wished to die, but when death is right before my eyes, I'd wish not to die.

It leaps again towards me and I close my eyes waiting for impact. My situation is not where someone comes and saves me, no I feel it grab my arm with its razor sharp teeth tearing through my flesh.

I scream as loudly as I can feeling the metallic smell of my own blood immediately through my nostrils. It grabs my neck scratching it carelessly, blood drips through the wounds on my body

I lay on the cold soil feeling myself weakening as it continues with its torture and it hurts so much. Pain is all I feel. I feel my breath come out in short pants as if I'm about to die which I think is true.

I close my eyes welcoming my on coming death with open arms. I'd always wanted to die at some point in my life and I've actually gotten my wish. I know I'd said before that death is not always the solution but I had thought about it anyway.

I didn't even realize that the beast had left me to die. Its main thing to do is kill. No not because you are its next meal or anything, its just an animal instinct.

You wonder why I didn't defend myself, its because I got no fighting skills at all and if I we're to fight it, my death would have been much more worst than before. I haven't shifted in along while, since the alpha banned me from doing so, so I prefer to die as peaceful as being ripped apart by argue can get.

I lay in my own pool of blood as my eyes keep shutting due to the amount of pain coursing through my body and it hurts alot. I barely feel any part of my body.

I wonder if anyone even heard my pleas for help. I shut my eyes again, I can still see but not strongly since my werewolf senses are already dull.

Suddenly heavy footsteps echo's through the already still night offering me a ray of hope that maybe I wouldn't die that maybe I'd still have my revenge even though both death and life are option worth trying because they'd be a reason for each one of them.

I'd wish to live for revenge, to see him beg me to forgive him while his whole face is bloody and hideous. On the other hand, I'd wish to die, to let go of everything that had ever hurt me and feel happy just to rest.

Suddenly gigantic boots comes into my line of vision, I look up slightly from where I'm lying and I'm met with a pair of cold looking brown eyes. I gasp slightly seeing the long thick scar from his left cheek all the way to his right cheek.

He stares at me emotionlessly as if waiting for me to die. My eyes begin to shut again but I feel this is different, that the next time I'd open them, I either be alive or dead.

And you know what?

I gave in and shut them.

Chapter 4

I woke up early today. I didn't want the alpha to wake me up with his crude methods that usually leave scars all over my body.

I'd either wake up feeling hot water being poured on my face or being hit by a whip and I swear its not pretty.

I walk to towards the kitchen which is dead silent since no one is awake yet. I stagger slightly considering I had not eaten anything last night.

He said I was three minutes late on bringing their meals. I offered a thankyou which he said was necessary to him and headed back to my bed.

I grab the rail stepping on the last steps and entering the gigantic kitchen. I am a slave to them, not worth it.

Thank goddess they never raped me or anything of the sort. Its the only thing that I still hold dear and can call mine. Today was the day I was going to shift. I'm already sixteen and my wolf would appear. I pray hard to the goddess to give me a wolf even though the chances of having one are so slim.

I sigh grabbing cooking pans and immediately starting my tiresome job. That's how my life works, work work and more work. I could say I'm used to it but I'm not.

Its still physically tiring. I swallow hard feeling my throat parched and I'm in desperate need of water. I grasp one of the glasses pouring myself a glass of water.

I take an enormous sip still holding the glass. My hands are trembling so much due to the lack of food that the glass slips from my hand before hitting the floor and shuttering into pieces.

My heartbeat picks up seeing the mess I just created. He will surely hurt me. He always does.

"What did you do?! " Someone snarps behind me and I don't need to turn around to see who it is for I already felt it in my bones.

"S-s-sorry A-alpha i-it w-was an a-a-accident." I stutter pathetically.

His face contorts into a snarl as his eyes flash gold meaning I wouldn't escape this. Its too early and I'm already getting a beating.

Before I know it he is standing next to me a murderous look in his eyes that promises me an oncoming pain. I prepare my body for I know theres no escaping it anyway. Its my fate.

He grabs me by my biceps pulling me to the torture room. A room I'm too familiar with. Just because I don't have my parents anymore. They made me a slave and there's nothing I can do about it.

I don't resist for it only makes my beating worse. He always has this horrible mood in the morning and I'm sure this is not going to end well for me.

He drags me down before chaining me to the wall. I'm used to this. He brings his favorite torture device which is a whip.

He doesn't speak, he just grabs the whip and hits my already sore back from bending too much.

He brings the whip to my back and hits me so hard that I scream out just on the first hit. I'm used to this but it doesn't make it any less painful.

He repeats the process a couple of times, until he is sweating. He unties me and I fall to the ground. He gives me a harsh glare before walking away.

He rarely talks when he's hurting and destroying me. He is my nightmare And I'd never forgive him. I sigh wiping the few tears that managed to escape my blood shot eyes.

This shouldn't discourage me, its my birthday and I'll meet my wolf. Maybe she'd show up even though I'm in alot of pain.

I smile to myself as more tears blur my eyes. I hate being weak and him being strong. I wish I was strong but I'd always been me.

I prepare breakfast after wiping all the blood off my body and wearing a clean pair of old clothes.

I wince each time I accidentally brush my hand on my back but I could so feel it healing up abit more quickly. Weird.

The pack members get in all of them taking their sits not bothering to say anything to me. I'm just a servant anyway and its high time I accept it.

They eat as I stare as them feeling the familiar growling of my stomach. I leave the room heading out, I don't want to be shoved or hit.

I sigh walking towards the trees feeling the cold soil between my toes. My badly injured back heals us slowly but surely. I know that even if it heals he is still just going to hurt me anyway. He always does.

Its only a matter of time before my healed wounds open up again and he'd repeat the process over and over again.

After walking for about twenty minutes to nowhere in particular trying to distract my tormented mind from recalling each and every painful experience in my life, I walk back to the pack house knowing they've completed eating.

Within a short period of time, I'm already standing outside the pack house. I rush in ready to wash the awaiting dishes, before I start preparing lunch for everyone.

My day went well lifeless if i can call it that anway, and I guess luck was on my side since I didn't encounter the alpha. I sigh with relief as I serve the last plate.

My wolf wouldn't show anymore since I would have already felt her. I get into the kitchen stealing some little leftover food and dashing towards my room avoiding being seen by anyone.

I eat savoring the delicious taste of the rare meal in my mouth since it would take some time before I get a delicious meal once again.

After eating, I rest my head on my mattress that can hardly be calls that anymore. Within few minutes I'm consumed by sleep.

I don't know if I even slept because I woke up with a burning sensation all over my body. I gasp for air feeling suffocated. what's wrong with me?

It doesn't take long before it dawns on me that maybe I'm shifting. My parents had told me about shifting and how amazing it is but being young they had failed to mention how painful it is.

After hours of endless torture and pain where I muffled my scream by shoving my old tee shirt in my mouth. I wouldn't want the alpha to wake up for he'd surely kill me for disturbing his peaceful sleep.

I could feel every crack of my bones as it resonated through my body. Every inch of my breaking bones, I felt each pain for there was no one to help me with it.

It took hours for the shift to end but the outcomes we're something I'd repeat again. I stood on all four as I trodded over to my mirror on my tiny bathroom.

I stared at my mesmerizing reflection. I had grey fur, white spots littered on mypaws. My eyes were a bright blue making me look more beautiful. I stared at my wolf in awe. It was totally worth it.

She told me how to shift back and for the first time in my life I was actually happy. I slept well knowing that nothing would ruin my mood.

The following morning, I woke up early started my normal duty and for once I had a small smile on my face and when I looked in the mirror my eyes had some shine to it that I thought I had lost years ago. I know everyone could tell by my scent that I had shifted.

As I was preparing the last pancake and carrying to the table, I collided hard with someone and I nearly fell down

Looking up I see Anabelle the alpha's sister, her face contorted in nothing but disgust as she stares at me.

"Watch where you are going you idiot," She snarls baring her teeth at me and for once I was feeling courageous that I decide to reply.

"You should watch where you are going instead of snapping at me and yelling at me for no apparent reason." I utter and her eyes widen in surprise. That was the worst mistake of my life.

She raises her hand up for a strike and I snap my eyes shut waiting for a strike only, it doesn't come.

I crack them open seeing an evil glint in her eyes. She drops her hand and walks off. I nearly smile victoriously but I felt something off with her calm nature and my question was answered minutes later.

The alpha storms into the kitchen with a sobbing Anabelle behind her. She set it all up.

Anabelle shoots a smirk towards me and I gulp knowing that whatever she said to him, would earn me a beating that would not end well.

"You ungrateful slut!! HOW DARE YOU INSULT ME, I AM YOUR ALPHA AND YOU SHOULD LEARN YOUR PLACE, YOU ARE NOTHING BUT TRASH THAT I CAN EASILY DISPOSE!! " He snarls as he grabs the hem of my blouse and drags me out of the kitchen.

He drags me to the torture room that I've grown accustomed to. He said that for him to prove how powerful he is he would leave a reminder on my face, he'd leave his mark and he sure did.

He grabs a silver knife and even though I have shifed, it would leave a scar. He takes it out and permanently scar my face. He dragged the knife on my right cheek to my left one.

My screams echoes through the mansion as I cry for help and as always no one comes. I am left with the beast. He orders me never to shift ever again and the second time I did, I nearly died due to the amount of pain I felt.

The only thing I recall as he was damaging my face was his genuine smile stretched on his lips and how his eyes were filled with amusement and sheer pleasure.

Chapter 5

My eyes shoot open and I inhale deeply trying to erase the memories that of that night. My hand unconsciously trace the scar on my face feeling the tiny bumps on my skin. The intricate scarring that he left there. The pure disgust I feel for him.

I clench my teeth as tightly as possible trying to erase their disgusting faces in my mind. Before my mind can drift any further, everything that happened storms my mind and I shut my eyes tight feeling my head pounding hard and my breath coming out in short quick pants.

I stare at my body that is wrapped in white bandages with a few spots leaking blood. My neck that had been scratched and almost broken looks as good as new with almost no signs of what occured previously.

Why am I not dead?

Once more the image of the emotionless black eyed guy pop into my mind making my breath hitch. Who was he and where am I?

My eyes scan the room, taking in the light blue colored walls and the queen sized bed I'm currently laying on. One night stand occupied the side of the bed with a post lamp next to it. There are two doors to the far right of the room and I presume its a bathroom and a closet. I step out of the bed in a hurry, and a galaxy of stars shoots through my eyes as I stumble and nearly tumble to the carpeted floor. To stop the fall, I fall back onto the bed.

A few minutes later and I cautiously repeat the action and manage to get out of the bed and step towards the door. Whoever brought me here must want to hurt me.

I creak the door open ready make my escape and get out of here. When I do, my breath sticks to my throat as the guy from that night stares at me with the same emotionless dark eyes.

We make eye contact and I avert mine away from his. I can the burning of his gaze on the side of my face. I fidget with the oversized blouse that I realize is currently draped over my body. It's too big reaching over my thighs. I can also feel a soft material on my legs and I look down and stare at the clean pair of sweatpants. Who changed me? Did the guy do it? That creeps me out a little bit.

I look up and meet his dark eyes and they harden even further and I almost flinch at the look. Without uttering a word, he storms out slamming the door shut almost giving me a heart attack. I vaguely see him carrying some bandages and disinfectant wipes. Did he take care of me? Why did he save me and what's with the intense glares?

I sigh and head back to bed. How am I supposed to get out of here? How am I even alive. I was so sure I'll die. I glance back at the white bandages adorning almost every inch of my body. I almost look like a mummy. The guy looks so dangerous and scary and I have no idea how he'd react to me wanting to leave. How and why did he save me?

I get in to the bathroom not trusting my smell since I cannot tell how long I've been here. Basing off my barely aching body, I can bet I have been unconscious for a long while. I lift my hand and slightly sniff my armpit and I nearly gag at the smell. That is so gross. Totally didn't think that through. I've seen people do it in movies.

I peal off my clothes and take the bandages off my flesh. I stare at the bloody mess that is my body and almost cringe at the sight. Most of the wounds I sustained having almost healed off except for the on my arm that is still painful. They leave a few white scars in it's wake. My hand runs through my shoulder that has a rather large scar. A quick flash of how it happened races through my mind. That disgusting man called a mate. Of course.

I run a bath for myself and rush in, a sigh rushing out of my lips in bliss. An hour later, my skin has started to prune and my arm begins to ache. I get out feeling much much better. Wrapping myself in a clean white towel, I exit the bathroom and head to the closet that is actual a walk in one.

A small gasp escapes my lips as I stare wide eyed at the amount of clothes all well organized in rows that I'm even ashamed to grab one with my filthy hands. After contemplating on what to wear, I grab one that looks quite cheap and worn.

The dress is an ugly dark blue color that has a bare back and short sleeves. It's knee length with a few fake diamonds littering the waist. It doesn't even conceal the scars and wound on my body. I don't dwell on it as I walk out of the room.

I take slow steps down the stairs, paying close attention to any sound that might be the guy. My sensitive hearing doesn't pick any sound and I sigh in relief as I walk more confidently down the stairs.

My eyes finds the door leading out and I almost sigh in relief. I take steps towards it, a smile forming on my lips. The light shinning through the door making me realize I'm right. I grab the handle and--

"Were do you think you're going?" A squeal rushes out of my mouth, as I turn around my eyes meeting his. The cold and ruthless orbs trained on me.

"How? How did you? " I stutter my mouth on the floor. I did not even hear him.

"What are you wearing?!" He growls staring at the ugly piece of fabric covering my body. His eyes burning through every inch of me.

"A dress?" It comes out as a question.

"Take it off." My eyes drop open.

Why would I take it off? Does he want. . . No, he doesn't look like a pervert.

Or maybe I'm wrong.

"W-what?" I stutter feeling tears gather in my eyes for no reason.

"I said take it off." He growls as he takes steps closer to me. I unconsciously takes many back, fear flooding my sense. Did I escape an abusive man only to land on another?

"W-why?" I stutter, scared out of my mind.

"It's so f-- ugly, get something else to wear." He grits out his cold emotionless eyes trained on the piece.

An uncontrolled sigh rushes out of my mouth. He doesn't want to take advantage of me.

He glare becomes even more intense me, eyes having no trace of any emotions leaving me confused even further.

"What did you think I was going to do?" He asks, his brow shooting to his hair, eyes focused on mine.

"You know... " I murmur and I feel my cheeks heat at my assumptions.

A short cold cackle leaves his mouth and I cringe away from him, my eyes widening, mouth dropping open.

"Don't fool yourself little girl, I don't rape women. You better keep that in mind. " He mutters his voice oozing anger and rage. "Take this." He grumbles handing me bandages and walking away. My mouth slightly opens as I stare at his retreating figure. Why would he help me? Why would he do it? I'm so confused.

Maybe he wants to use me too like the rest of that pack. Like the ex mate? I refuse to dwell on him. O. That disgusting past. I sigh grabbing the hem of my dress before going back to the room I was in before. It looks like I'm stuck here for now.

Getting in, I grabbed an oversized shirt and a pair of sweat pants which surprisingly fit me well, before flopping down on the bed.

What am I going to do to get out of here? Just the thought of living together or staying close to such an emotionless guys send chills down my spine. I have to find a way out of here and I have to find it fast.

Chapter 6

Pain fills every cell of my body as I keep going with the unsteady punches on the punching bag. I can feel how bruised and broken my knuckles are from the vigorous and rather uncoordinated punched I'm throwing on the bag. My mind is however not focused on it. My mind goes back to her. The woman I have hurt and found pleasure in her tears. How could I possibly do that to the one person I was meant to love, to cherish and treat right. How could I?

The look on her face still makes my heart shatter into a million pieces. Never in my wildest dreams would I have thought that her, the pack servant, the orphan would turn out to be my mate. The mate I have spent almost four years searching. The same mate I swore to never hurt when I witnessed my father abusing his. My mother.

Two toxic mates who caused enough scars to my sister and I. The same mates who found pleasure in hurting us. I had swore never to hurt mine and here I am, almost killing mine.

The mere thought of all the torture I put her through eats my soul, tearing and breaking me. The rage I feel makes me want to break something. I caused her anguish, her pain and grief.

I sigh realizing that whatever I'm doing isn't helping at all. I stop and walk away from the punching bag, my feet leading me unconsciously to her room, her sweet scent invading my nostrils.

I take steps down the stairs to her room, a horrible looking room with barely maintained condition. I had never really cared, she was just another she wolf who meant nothing and I never minded at all. In fact I enjoyed seeing her cower, seeing tears trail down her cheeks as she shivered in fear.

I fed off her fear and each time she was near me I would make sure she knew her place, she was beneath me and that's where she would always belong, well that's until that day I nearly took advantage of her. The day I almost forced myself on her.

The memories of that night keeps playing in my mind and giving me nightmares of when she doesn't escape and I have my way, I stab her, I rape her and she. . .dies.

I wake up drenched in sweat regretting each and everything I did. It always felt wrong. I always felt it wasn't right but I loved it. I loved when she cowered in fear. When she cries out in pain, when she begged me to stop and I enjoyed the pain in her eyes as they stared up at me pleading.

Just the thought of all the things she has gone through saddens me, breaks me, destroys me. I let it all happen, I let my mate get beaten. What if she had been raped before? What if I was among guys who had taken advantage of her? What if it's not only me who took advantage of her?

The thought of it makes me so angry yet I can't reverse time. I can't go back to the past and change and recreate our lives.

I slam my hand at a nearby object which happens to be a mirror and it shatters into pieces. That's how I broke her. I shattered her. Each time I hit her, I whipped her, I tore a part of her and I loved every second of it.

I grit my teeth, clenching my fist tight as I storm out of the room not willing to see the poor state of it any further. I exit the pack house, pack members staring at me their fear barely concealed.

I understand why. I have turned cold this past few months making me cold and unapproachable. I walk out my lips thinning as I shoot a freezing glare at anyone staring at me making them cower and scurry off.

When I am far from the pack house, I let out an enormous roar for everything I have done wrong, for everything that I made her go through, things I can never reverse or undo.

What if she had not turned as my mate? What if I had killed her that night when she came? I drop to my knees forcing myself to shift into my wolf.

When you force a shift, it hurts more than even the first shift. I grit my teeth as the first bone pop. I keep chanting in my mind that I deserve this, I deserve this more than anything, I hurt my other half.

The second bone pop making me groan in pain. Everything, every pain that I had caused her flash through my eyes, every hit, every slap, every taunting and disgusting words I threw her way.

I close my eyes as the pain gets unbearable and I let out a scream as I fall on my side as more bones pop as I morph into my wolf.

My vision starts to fade at the amount of pain I was feeling. I kept repeating the same words. I deserve it.

My eyes goes blurry as more black spots appear. I pray and beg that she comes back, just like some of my pack members whose mate would leave and come back looking more beautiful than when they left.

I wish my story was as cliche as that, that she will show up and I will apologize for everything I did to her, for hurting her but I know, deep down, that when she does show up it won't be how I expect it to be.

With that thought everything around me fades and I plunge into the darkness.

Chapter 7

I can't sleep. I keep tossing and turning on my bed trying to find a comfortable position. I groan opening my eyes softly before swinging my legs and getting out of bed.

I have not seen the nameless guy all day today and I couldn't be happier. Avoiding him was even harder since we lived in the same house. I sigh walking down the stairs rubbing my eyes softly.

I walk over to the pantry rubbing my arms as I stared wondering what to pick up. Before I can choose, loud groans and weird noises echos through the empty house. What the hell?

I creepily tiptoed towards the noise, knowing pretty well that if it's a rogue or something, I can kiss my sorry life goodbye.

I walk over to a barely lit room. I crack the door open slowly and make my way in. I didn't actually prepare for the sight in front of me.

The creepy guy whom I needed to name, punching a bag. His muscles out for display. I stare at his toned body my eyes widening at how perfect he looks. His breathing coming out quick yet he looks composed. I would be dead by now if I was the one doing that.

He keep going at it graciously as I stare in awe. Even warriors in my previous pack didn't do such training. I know this is kind of creepy staring shamelessly at a guy who doesn't even know I'm here.

My eyes we're solely fixed on his muscles that kept clenching each time he hits the bag. Even my wolf was somehow enjoying it as much as I was.

I should definitely lose sleep each night if I'm going to see him like this. Even the scar on his face makes him look hot. I usually thought scars made people less attractive but he looks perfect. My hand goes to my own scar. Does it make me attractive too or do I sc-

"What are you doing here?" He asks his voice gruff and I immediately snap out of my thoughts as I stare at him. Cold emotionless eyes, again.

"I couldn't sleep. I didn't know you had a gym." I reply walking in and staring at all the equipments he had. He doesn't answer my question, instead he goes back to punching the bag that I now realize he had stopped.

He keeps going at it ignoring me completely. I roll my eyes as I walked out not really feeling comfortable with the emotionless guy who could easily kill me.

I walked towards my room not in the mood for food anymore. I flop down hoping that somehow I get sleep and almost immediately my eyelids begin to droop as I fell asleep.

I swallowed hard as I walked towards the alpha's office. He had summoned me once again today.

I knocked his door tapping my foot impatiently on the floor as I bit my nail fear clouding my entire being. I receive a come in as I push the door open.

I walked in my head solely kept down my eyes trained on the floor. I could feel the erratic beatings of my heart. I dreaded coming here. Whenever I came here I always, always ended up with a scar somewhere in my body.

"Why are you late." He growls out rage evident in his voice causing my body to stiffen in absolute fear as my hands clench tight as I try to control them from shaking and I was definitely doing a poor job at it.

"I'm sorry Alpha." I murmur in a barely audible voice as hot tears form in my eyes at the thought of what he'd do to me.

I didn't know my mistake today and I just had to accept it because everyone in this pack had made it their duty to lie to the alpha as log as I somehow ended up in pain. The reasons for this actions is still unknown to me.

"Did you insult the beta female?" He snaps and I could almost feel him losing control. Ah the beta female. She wanted me to clean her huge mansion and I couldn't since I had other duties that I needed to attend to.

"N-no A-Alpha." I whisper in fear as my heart beats harder and harsher against my chest feeling the familiar constricting feeling as black spots flood my vision.

He could hear my heartbeats and I know he thinks I'm lying. When a wolf lies or anyone else, their heart beats increase signifying they are lying.

My case was different though. My heart was beating erratically because I was sure I was going to get punished anyway. My heart was beating rapidly because I had no idea what pain he would instill on me today.

Without any warning, he launches himself at me and before I could actually comprehend it. He had me by my neck by the wall.

"You bitch! How dare you lie to me. I'm your Alpha!"he growls out in absolute rage as his fist connects with my stomach in pain.

I hissed in pain as I kept my head bowed not willing to meet his eyes that I was sure were a darker shade.

"I'm sorry alpha." I whisper harshly my chest constricting harder at the lack of oxygen. He hold on my neck gets harder and I was definitely sure it would leave a huge scar as his nails digged deeper onto my skin.

He growls out in rage as his fist continuously connects with my stomach, face, hands. Every part of my body.

"Please... stop." I gasp in pain as he keeps going ignoring my pleads. He suddenly lets go of my neck and my head connects with the floor as tears rapidly fall put of my eyes.

He doesn't stop, instead he hits me harder, using his feet to kick me harder.

"Please...I can't take it anymore... Alpha... please stop." My voice comes out in a whisper as my vision starts to blur in unbelievable pain. I could feel my body growing numb in absolute and utter pain.

I could feel my breath growing short and breathing getting more labored. I hear the prominent crack of my ribs. My eyes roll back and my vision darkens and I welcome the inevitable darkness.

A horrifying scream leaves my lips as I immediately sit up on my bed. I could feel sweats dripping down my back and my hair clamped together by sweats.

I laid down trying to control my breath that was coming put harshly. Even though I'm not with them, they control my dreams, they take my peace.

The little sanity that I try to hold on to slips through my hands each time. I try so hard to feel okay. I try so hard to try and be normal,only normalcy isn't a word for me anymore. That word doesn't exist in my life anymore.

Without my consent or control, tears immediately drip down my face in absolute terror and pain. I hiccup in pain as memories that I try so so hard to keep down floods my mind.

I clench my hand tightly feeling the need to destroy the stupid pack, the need to destroy my so called mate, to feel him writhing in nothing but pain till he is begging for me to stop just like how I did so many times.

Instead I felt so weak and utterly defenseless like how I've felt all my life. I let the tears fall again, fall because of them. I could try and promise myself that this would be the last time I did but I am absolutely sure it wasn't.

Chapter 8

"**M**ama! Mama! Can you tell me how you and Papa met?" I ask my voice low as I stare up with my huge doe eyes at my smiling mother.

"But Amore! I've told you this story so many time presiozo." She whispers as she scoops me in her arms placing me securely on her lap as she presses a gentle kiss on my forehead and hair.

"But I love it Mama!" I whine giving her a puppy look and she sighs rolling her eyes at me small frame.

"That's cheating," she mumbles mostly to herself as she stares down at my small frame on her lap.

"Okay fine," she agrees and I squeal loudly, bouncing slightly on her lap. She rolls her eyes at my antics but still smiles nonetheless.

"Back in my pack, my father was a pack..."

A loud scream echoes through the house and I shoot out of bed nearly breaking my neck as the duvet covers tangle my legs in a tight twist. I look around frantically wondering where the scream came from.

I slowly untangle myself from my covers as I peek outside before stepping out of my room, walking aimlessly. After walking around for a few minutes, my mind registers what I'm doing. I think I just love getting myself in trouble. I should go back to my room before I come face to face with that...that creep. I turn ready to go back but halt when my ears pick up heavy breathing in a room right in front of me.

Without thinking about it, I push the door slightly and not to my surprise it's open. I peek in and my eyes widen at the sight before me. The emotionless guy sprawled out on his bed, his hand clutching his head tightly. I watch before my eyes, as a tear drop down his cheeks, and his eyes...his eyes that have always been so emotionless held one emotion, just one that nearly hurt me too;pain, unbelievable amount of pain.

A new feeling shoots through my chest as I stare at him. I suddenly get the urge to walk over to him and engulf him in a hug but I'm sure I'd just make everything worse and I might just end up dead. Without uttering a word, I close the door as lightly as possible before wobbling back to my room.

The image of the guy comes back to my mind and my mind race endlessly with questions. Why did he look so hurt? So much pain. I get into my warm bed wondering what made him that hurt. I had nearly judged him. No wonder his so cold. He too went through something and the only way to protect himself is to stay cold and lock down each and every emotion he has. It's the only way for him not to hurt or feel. It's understandable. He's usually so emotionless with this dark aura around him that makes me avoid him like a plague, and now I somehow understand.

He's just like me, scarred by his past, made emotionless and cold. I turn a couple of times trying to get his image out of my head, only it doesn't work. Thought after thought keeps running through my mind and I immediately knew that I was not going to sleep.

The light rays of the sun streamed through the thick curtains of my room, slightly lighting everything up. Just like I had thought, I didn't get any ounce of sleep and I'm pretty sure I was a creepier version of The walking Dead. I unfold the warm duvet from my body, immediately being hit by the cold hair causing several goosebumps appear on my skin. I trod over to the bathroom and my presumption are confirmed as I stare at the heavy circles under my eyes.

I walk into the shower stripping and turning on the water. I let the warm water cascade down my back and a heavy sigh leaves my lips as tiredness leaves me temporarily. I search through the drawers, finding an unused toothbrush and toothpaste. Twisting the toothpaste open, I press some of it onto the brush, vigorously brushing my teeth and rinsing my mouth with the water.

I walk out of the bathroom walking over to the walk in closet, picking another set of clothes before putting them on. I really should leave, I mean I'm already feeling fine. After dressing, I walk out towards the kitchen in search of food.

Heavy scent of coffee lingers in the air as I walk further down the stairs. I walk into the kitchen and I nearly gasp as I stare at the guy whom I need to find a name for preparing pancakes.

"Hey," I offer and nearly smacking myself hard at the weird greeting I just gave him. He doesn't even turn and my cheeks nearly burn when I realize he wasn't going to reply. I was almost ready to turn and walk away but I make out a slight grunt from him and i just sigh taking it as a reply not really caring if he was actually replying or because of his own personal issues. I don't ponder further on it because suddenly a questions I've been dying to know the answer to flood my mind and before I can stop it, it leaves my lips.

"Why did you save me?" My eyes trained on his now rigid form by the cooker. I stare at his back, trying hard to ignore the prominent flexing of his muscles by his movements. Just like how I anticipated, he's quiet and for once, I get angry.

I walk over to him, grabbing his arm ,and pulling him so he's staring at me.

"What's wrong with you?! I keep talking to you and all you do is shut up as if you can't actually talk?! It's tiring you know. If you aren't going to answer me, I'm gonna match through that door and I swear..." I stop mid sentence as the dark aura around him grows even darker. I take a step back, my eyes trained on his face. His face is just as emotionless like the first time I saw him but his eyes are dark, nearly black. His jaw clenched tightly that I thought it would break, his hands clenched in a tight fist that even his knuckles had turned white.

My face pales at the sight. I had never seen him this mad before and I immediately regret my words. His eyes still focused on me, narrows into slits and I audibly gulp in fear.

"Get out," he utters almost calmly that I nearly missed it.

"W-what?" I question my brows scrunched in nothing but confusion.

"I said get out!" He snaps and I flinch back as terror washes over my body and without my consent, I begin shaking like a frail leaf. A sudden memory surface and I immediately turn around racing back to the room I was a couple of minutes ago.

I rush in slamming the door shut and slide down on the floor tears already falling. I felt disgusted by myself. I hated myself at this particular moment and not because I didn't get the courage to ask him why he saved me. I hated myself because I became a coward and ran. That's what I always do, run, for it's the only thing I know. It's what I've always done and I did it again.

Chapter 9

I tiptoed out of the room making sure that my steps were as light as humanly possible. I twisted my head both sides, enhancing my hearing abilities trying to make out some peculiar noises. A deep sigh escapes my lips as I slightly turned the door knob before stepping out into the cold harsh night.

After the guy had harshly glared at me and threw harsh words my way, I was cooped up in the room that I had currently branded as my own. I had stayed in and actually didn't get out, only when I was really hungry.

What he actually said made me think really hard about why I was still stuck here. I appreciate everything he did for me, I really do but when he started acting like a total asshole, all the gratitude I had for him disappeared like it never existed.

I, for once did a happy dance finally acknowledging the fact that I was finally outside and I could finally escape. My victory was short-lived as I stared at the pitch black house beside me. Though lights surrounded each part of this magnificent house, further away was black pitch and I couldn't stop a shiver that ran down my spine.

To be honest, I've always been afraid of the darkness because I knew and believed that during this time, it was actually when demons and our worst fears arose. It scared me to no end, honestly.

Inhaling sharply, I began my journey towards the dark tall trees that surrounded the house. I could help but gulp audibly as I stared at the darkest part of the trees. Grasping my chest tightly, I kept on walking hoping that I actually manage to get through and escape. Escape to where you ask. That I don't know but I was willing to go further from the terrifying guy.

Swallowing harshly, I kept walking with totally no sense of direction. I enhance my werewolf vision and yet I still couldn't see well. My heart begins pounding so rapidly against my chest that and I was almost passing out. Stumbling over fallen branches and stones, I kept walking trying to ignore the fact that I was petrified of the dark, petrified of what could happen to me.

I don't know for how long i walked, but then suddenly a though came to me. What was thinking anyway walking out at night randomly and claiming I wanted to escape. It's no use actually no use. I could turn back and try and find my way back to the house or keep tumbling and get attacked with rogues and I was definitely sure that this time I wouldn't be so lucky to be saved. It's obvious what choice I made though. Even though I really truly want to escape, I can't do it when I have no idea where I am or where exactly I'm heading.

It's now I'm realizing how dumb I am acting. Why would I randomly wake up and decide to escape? Turning back, I try to see if I can try and find that gigantic house which I was in a while ago and I nearly scream in fear at how dark it was. Everything was beyond dark and this made me question how long I had been walking.

My heart that was beating rapidly gets wild as I create scenarios of what would happen to me here. I would either get eaten by rogues, or captured by hunters or maybe a mad scientist who would use me as an experiment and finally find werewolves and it would be the end of the world. That's a bit wild but right now I was freaking out.

I kept turning in each and every direction until my head was finally a jumble mess and I couldn't recall where I came from or where I was heading. I then decided that I would just walk in any random direction and this actually confused me more.

When I realized I wasn't going to get back, my chest began constricting from lack of air. I inhale deeply trying to get in as much oxygen as I could but it wasn't walking. I kept inhaling only it wasn't enough. Making out a tree, I head over it before leaning and heaving so harshly. Falling down on my knees, I pull my legs to my chest, my chest still constricting.

I hadn't even noticed how my vision had faded until everything turned dark and I lost consciousness.

Chapter 10

I came to with a jolt, my heart pounding so fast against my chest that I nearly passed out again. Grasping my chest tightly, I titled my head both sides trying to decipher where the hell I was. The bright rays made it's way to my face and immediately winced before squinting my eyes as a groan left my lips.

Turning both sides, I crawled up before standing straight. I can't believe I'm still in the same position I was the previous night. I barely recall passing out at some point in the night due to all the fear and weird and unreasonable thoughts that had me trapped.

Twisting my head left to right through the thick trees I try to find the house I was in a couple of hours ago. I turn left and immediately my eyes widen in both shock and anger. About half mile from where I was, the beautiful mansion stood majestically staring and taunting me. I had not even wondered off that far yet I couldn't see.

Groaning loudly, I begin hittimg my head slightly against a nearby tree before instantly regretting it as waves of pain shoot through my head. Why didn't I see the mansion before? I mean it's even visible from where I'm standing?

Shaking my head, I erase all those thoughts just thankful that I had not strayed so far from it. Walking hurriedly, I headed back to the house still in shock.

I did another happy dance because one, I wasn't dead and two, I was back to the mansion. I better be trapped with an emotionless guy than to get trapped by a rogue who'll for sure feed of my flesh.

Walking closer to the door, I twist the door knob and pushing the door open and slamming it shut again as I shut my eyes, a deep sigh escaping my chapped lips. I shut out everything, just focusing on my breathing.

In my moment of rush I had not noticed the guy standing not far from me and that's why when I snapped my eyes open, a scream left my lips as I stared at his cold, bored and emotionless eyes.

"Are you trying to kill me?!" I snap clasping my hand so tightly against my racing heart. I wonder why I haven't gotten a heart attack already from all the fright and fear I've been getting and feeling. I immediately regret it as he sends me a harsh glare and my mind immediately goes back to the previous night and I wince.

"Sorry." I mutter lowly my eyes trained on my now muddy white vans that have turned a brown color and I am pretty sure I'm not wearing them anymore.

"Where were you?" He question in an utterly bored tone like just simply asking where I was was the most tiring thing ever. I couldn't tell him I was actually trying to escape. He'd throw me out for sure and from what I've learnt he's beyond emotionless and I don't want to cross the line.

"Did you try to escape?" He inquires,his voice coming out as bored and uncaring. I immediately chock on air. Why is he acting so casual about it and does he know? At this my heart begins pounding so hard.

"What...Pft...No?" I stutter out trying to convince both of us. I look up and I immediately flinch at the glare he was sending my way.

"I can hear you heart beating so rapidly." He calmly states as he narrows his eyes at me and I immediately give up, sighing deeply. Why did he even ask that? It's not like I am his prisoner or anythi ng...or am I?

"Look, I'm sorry okay. Yes I tried to escape but only because I couldn't stay here with you always glaring at me and barely showing any emotion. I would even get frightened at night thinking that maybe you'd attack me and kill me in my sleep. I even don't know your name! I mean who in their right mind stays with a complete stranger and be pretty comfortable with it. You saved my life and I truly appreciate it but we just can't keep ignoring each other each and everyday! I need to know why you saved me!" I exclaim before heaving in and out trying breath normally. That's the most sincere thing I've ever said in my whole life and I expected a reaction from him. Something like understanding, remorse or even regret. What I didn't expect though is a totally blank look and a clenched fist. Did I do something wrong again? I know I haven't so what's with him?

"Are you done?" He asks crossing his arms across his muscular chest and I struggle to ignore the clenching of his muscles. I imme-diately note what he said and my jaw drops. Really?! I've been so sincere here and that's what he has to say? Clenching my fist tightly, I suppress the urge to punch his face. Sighing deeply, I control my burning rage as I send a harsh glare his way.

"I hope you've learnt your lesson," he says still bored."I knew you wouldn't make it though."

At this confession my jaw drops to the floor and I blink. Once. Twice. He...he knew all along? Why didn't he stop me or even try to help me when I got lost? He watched the whole scenario? Something else in my mind clicks. Why couldn't I see the mansion yet I wasn't too far away from it?

"Why couldn't I see the mansion?" I ask staring at him and from he look on his face I know he knows exactly what I'm talking about.

"I switched off the lights." He calmly states still utterly bored. Instead of throwing a fit, I sighed deeply just trying to understand him. He's so cold and him doing that shouldn't be a surprise. He stares at me as if waiting for my reaction but I offer him nothing.

"Okay." I state lifting my head and staring into his cold eyes. His slightly widen in what I presume as surprise before going blank again. That's the only emotion he has ever showed me and I'm quite surprised he did.

"What is your name?" I suddenly ask because I was tired of branding him as the emotionless guy or cold eyes. He stares at me for a while before clenching his fist tightly sending. Okay bipolar much?

He sends me a harsh glare before walking towards me with steady slow steps. My eyes widen as I stare at his tall frame and his intimidating scar that occupies a large part of his handsome face. I unconsciously take a step back in nothing but fear and fright. My breathing picks up as his cold eyes meet with mine. I was ready to bolt but before I could, he utters one word before walking away and that widens my eyes and my jaw drops for the hundredth time.

"Christian."

Chapter 11

Christian? Christian. Christian. Christian. Really?

I don't know but I've always thought that Christian is named after someone who's so good and kind hearted. So to be honest, the name didn't suit him but I accepted to call him anyway. It's better than cold eyes or emotionless guy.

After my failed attempt to escape, I didn't try it again and to be honest I don't think I was going to do it again but I also was beyond bored here repeating the same routine each and every day. Waking up. Eat. Sleep. Repeat. It was actually draining me. I couldn't actually escape because, I didn't have anywhere to go and joining another pack was not an option and would never be. The thoughts of joining a pack sends waves of fear down my spine. Thinking of being controlled by another alpha is something that I'm not comfortable with.

My good mood immediately turns sour as thoughts of my previous alpha and mate flood my mind. I unconsciously trace the deep scar on my face as I grit my teeth in nothing but anger. Fate has not been fair to me to be honest and him being my mate was the final straw. All the things he did will never be forgotten or forgiven. All the abuse, the tears but most importantly, the pain. The pain I felt was so bad and for years I thought maybe one day it would stop. It didn't. I had to save myself from all that torture. No one cared that I was hurting. This deep gush in my chest would never fully heal, I was sure of that.

Even if by sheer luck or by some force I end up forgiving him, which was not going to happen anyway, the scar would forever be on my face and just knowing he's the one who placed it there, would be even more complicated.

My mom used to tell me when I was younger than our challenges and pain makes us stronger and it prepares us for something greater and up until now, I haven't had anything good come my way. In fact, I'm still in pain.

I swore the moment I left that pack that I'd have my revenge, yes I was angry when I said it but I meant each and every word. I'll make sure to destroy it. I'll watch is crumble and I'll enjoy each and every second of it.

A shiver runs down my body and I immediately realize that my water has turned cold on my bath tub. Getting up, I step out and immediately wrap a dry clean towel around my shivering form.

Walking out, I walk over the walk in closet and pick another set of clothes for myself. Dressing quickly, I walk down the stairs feeling a growl rumble in my stomach.

I head towards the kitchen in search of food. I poke my head into the fridge trying to find something I can eat.

Loud groans echoes through the still house and I halttrying to identify the source of the weird and peculiar noises.

Hasn't this happened before?

Tiptoeing just like before, I follow the noises. I'm almost sure it's just Christian again so I don't try to be very discreet about it.

The groans keeps getting louder as I reach a particular door that leads outside. My face scrunches up in confusion. Opening the door, I match out fighting the urge to yell out Christian's name.

Walking further into the deep forest that happens to be just behind the mansion, I follow the groans that had turned to growls. A weird feeling settles at the pits of my stomach.

Something was wrong. Something was very wrong.

My wolf kept growing, warning me not to take another step into the dense woods. I ignored the feeling, and kept walking further.

It doesn't take long for me to reach my destination and to regret it immediately. I stare wide eyed at the scene before me. Four wolves kept snarling at each other, each trying to kill the other.

I sniff the air and I tense.

Rogues.

They all had the crazed look in their eyes. Taking a step back, I decide to run back and inform Christian who I had not seen since last night.

But as always, luck hates me and I step on a dry branch and immediately all their heads snap to my direction. My eyes widen in pure fear.

I had faced rogues before and I wasn't ready for another stupid encounter. Without waiting for them to react, I sprint away using all the energy in me.

I could hear the snarls and snapping of teeth just behind me as they both tried to grab my legs or any other part of my body so they can kill me.

I wasn't ready to die yet and currently my life was flashing before my eyes.

I wonder though why I always attract danger? Why do I always have to get into trouble each time. Pushing myself harder, I keep running.

Before I could get any further, pain shoots through my ankle and immediately realize that one of them must have caught my ankle with it's razor sharp teeth.

My strength almost instantly depletes as the pain I felt before flows through my body and I fall down with a thud. Turning around, I growl lowly at the wolves surrounding me, saliva dripping continuously down their snouts.

I wasn't going to go down without a fight this time round. I would die taking taking one is not all of them.

One to my right growls loudly before taking the first leap at me. I crouch down and it misses me by an inch. The other rogues seeing this as an opportunity to attack, all do it at the same time making me even more vulnerable.

I dodge some bites and others manage to actually pull chunks of flesh for me. I needed to shift or I was going to die. But shifting is going to take more time and I lacked time.

Before I can actually make a life changing decision, a large and I mean large black wolf emerges from the depth snarling and showcasing its long fangs well positioned on it's jaw.

My strength and will to fight dies with it. I knew them that I wouldn't survive this. I can as well say goodbye to my pathetic excuse of a life.

I've suffered enough andaybe in my story I wasn't supposed to get a happy ending. I mean not all of us were meant to get that sweet happy ever aftet. That's how life is anyway.

All the rogues that had been attacking me turn their attention to the new wolf and they all begin growling at it. I stare at it in confusion trying to find a reason for their weird reaction.

That when a thought hit me. Maybe he's not on their side and I have a chance of surviving it all.

The brown wolf lets out a huge growl that shakes some nearby trees and also manages to shake me to the core. Before any of the wolves could react, the brown wolf had already pounced on them tearing each and everyone of them easily.

I gulp loudly as one of the rogue's head rolls towards me. I let out a scream as I scramble back, moving further away from the bloody body.

I lift my head up and stare directly at a pair of cold emotionless eyes. The wolf's eye.

Where have I seen those eyes before?

I don't think much because my eyes widen in recognition. Even in wolf form he manages to look so blank and so emotionless.

"Christian?" I find myself questioning him and he rolls his eyes. Yes I just saw him roll his wolf eyes. I stare at him questioningly. A smile stretches at my lips when I realize he saved me.

Staring up at him, I offer him a huge smile that actually reaches my eyes.

"Thank you for saving me, Christian." I offer with a smile, my eyes shining.

The crack of bones makes me smile disappear. His shift is so quick that the next thing I'm seeing is his naked form. He rises to his height and I let out a scream when I realize he's stark naked.

Before I can speak again, he snaps in pure anger and what I think is disgust.

"You're so weak! I thought you were gonna put up a fight those rogues. Apparently, you are just another stupid wolf with no strength. I bet that's why you have that stupid scar on your fucking face. Your pack must have seen how weak you are and decided to do that to you. What can I say? I think it really suits you." Christian says all at once staring at me with hate and malice.

My breath halts at how cruel his words are. It really hurt more than anything. A tear slides down my cheek as I look up and stare at him. He stares at me before scoffing and pushing past me not caring about his nakedness.

That was the least of my concern right now. My heart felt like it was being squeezed and I couldn't get enough oxygen to my constricting lungs.

He left me there crying my eyes out and wondering why I was still alive. Memories of my past flashes through my eyes and I square my shoulder knowing that I had gone through tougher things than his and I was not going to to let his words hurt me.

Well, it was easier said that done.

Chapter 12

I guess my life is more cliche than I anticipated. The number if times I've been attacked by a rogue had left me feeling drained.

I guess sometimes fate loves to mess with my life. Well when I escaped from that darn pack, I wanted freedom, peace, happiness that I lacked. Mostly I wanted revenge. I've talked about it more than once and honestly I wasn't even picturing myself achieving it.

Many things were hindering me from getting and the more I thought about it, the more I realized that maybe revenge was just a pigment of my imagination, just something to channel my anger to. That at the end of the day if still be the loser and they would have managed to walk away free.

The thought left a bitter taste in my mouth and I subconsciously clench my fist tighter. No one had ever really respected me. Not even Christian.

Well Christian's case is a lot complicated and harder. My mind keeps drifting back to that time, a week ago when he saved me from those rogues. I wanted then to believe that he had a heart. That beyond his cold nature, he somehow felt something.

Well I was proven wrong when he spoke those harsh words. I know they didn't sound so bad but when you've grown up being told your so worthless, a little hurt and the wounds you try to stitch together will all open up like a fresh wound.

Thinking about my life right now I realize that I had no purpose. All my life I've been pushed, tossed and rejected. Even though my mate didn't do it, he had rejected me a long time ago the moment he laid a finger on me.

Sobbing and mopping around won't help at all for eventually I will end up the loser. Thinking of my ex pack makes me so angry. While they all lived happily, I suffered carrying the burden of the idiotic pack. I have scars in places I'm so embarrassed about.

My life has always been miserable and I needed to change it. I need to teach that pack a lesson. Staring at myself currently I realised that I have nothing to offer.

I can't fight and I was nearly mauled by a rogue. How cliche that is. At that moment, like a light bulb, an idea pops in my head.

I'll train, I'll train so hard. I'll train and make sure that I become the best. I'm not training to be an assassin that would be spoken by the werewolf race. I'll train to get revenge not to show off. So damn cliche.

But I need it. I need to destroy them so I can finally find peace of mind. I had heard so much of she wolves who would get hurt by their packs and they could escape and later come back and embrace the pack. How naive are they.

Forgiveness is not like plucking flowers or something.

Forgiveness is forgetting, forgiveness means lettting go and moving on. I couldn't do that. They needed to understand that I wasn't an ordinary wolf. That forgiveness was no longer in me.

Well, maybe when I was younger but right now. I needed to let them know. I would die fighting them because even if I wouldn't win, I know I would have tried my best to break them like how they did me.

Clenching my fist, I slam it so hard against the wall, that I felt my knuckles slightly crack from all the pain. Swallowing the pain, I match out of the room knowing that things were going to change.

I was going to train and I definitely know of a perfect teacher. Even though he's so cold, I would have to do it for it's what I want.

Following his unique scent, I find him at the same place I found him. The gym.

"I need you to train me."

The moment I uttered those words, I knew there was no backing away from it and I know it's what I needed.

"Oh and before we start, my name is Ciane. I know you were never going to ask and I don't need you insulting me." I say with a new attitude for I realized for people to respect me, I needed to earn it, or instill it in them in form of fear. Well I prefer the latter.

With that, I just signed my death certificate with a cold hearted beast. It didn't take long for him to stop his motion as he stared at me with distaste. He gives me a once-over before going back to punching the bag.

"Hey did you hear me?" I yelled glaring at his muscles that kept clenching and the coat of sweat dripping down his back.

"I heard you loud and clear, Ciane." He muttered my name with so much distaste that I nearly hated my name too. I know he doesn't like me but can he just lower it a bit.

"You're not a worthy opponent or student." He says and my eyes widen in both surprise and anger. How dare he judge me so easily? How dare he makes such assumptions!

He doesn't know me and he has absolutely no right to judge me! I maybe be weak but that doesn't make me incapable of it.

"What? And how do you know that?!" I ask not trying to hide the annoyance in my voice from him as I glared so harshly at him.

"Oh, I can tell your so weak. I'm not just talking about the rogues. I'm talking about you personally. You are weak and soft. You are just not going to make it." He says finally stopping the assaults. I gape at him. Too weak and too soft?

How dare he? Sighing deeply, I swallow the rage that kept bubbling at the pits of my stomach. If he refuses to train me I'm never going to get my revenge back which is why I was doing this in the first place.

No he can't not train me! I need him. I guess the realisation finally dawned on me.

"What must I do to prove my self worth." I ask through clenched teeth. I ask as I stare at his figure as he gulped down the water from a water bottle.

He takes a few gulps before staring into my eyes, a dark glint appearing there.

"Are you sure about this, girl?" He asks amusement dancing in his eyes and this even ticks me off. Through clenched teeth, I respond.

"Of course I am!" He sighs before smirking devilishly and I immediately know I'm in trouble. He utters the words and I gape at him, my jaw dropping in pure horror at what he said.

Chapter 13

"GET me an Agomi flower," he replied is voice nothing but sincere yet devoid of any known emotion. My eyes like saucers began to widen as I stared at him in utter shock.

"A- Agomi flower?" I stuttered, my breath sticking to my throat as I repeated the question.

He only glanced at me, his dark eyes narrowing at me. However, my shock was beyond justified. Agomi flowers are the rarest of them all, the only flower that is able to completely take a wolf's ability to shift.

A legend. Something my mother had read out to me when I had accidentally found the book, talking all about them.

"Oh my goddess. You know Agomi flowers do not exist! They were wiped out during the wolf War." I stated, my eyes still fixed on his that even it it were possible, narrowed on mine even further.

"In other words, this training ain't happening, little girl." The pure insult from those words didn't deter me though for finally, once in my life, I wanted something. For once I was willing to struggle to get it.

"Please, Christian. Please I would do anything for you to teach me, please." I pleaded, sounding pathetic and weak. Just as how I felt within anyway.

His eyes snap to meet mine once again in a heated glare. I had to push down the urge to scoff and insult him. However, when I noted his sudden interest did I finally realize what I've decided. I would do anything to be able to fix my past. To take my vengeance on that pack that had stolen so much from me.

"Anything?" I knew my answer and with absolute no hesitation, I replied.

"Yes, Christian. Anything." I confirmed.

However, soon a smile I had never seen on his lips brightened his entire face. I was in for trouble and I realized that.

"Training starts tomorrow at exactly 5.00am. Don't be late." He said, and my smile begins to crawl back to my lips. However, I suddenly remember promising him to do anything and I find myself yelling for him.

"Christian! So what am I supposed to do. What do you want from me that is a replacement for my training,"

He almost halts on his steps but before I could even note it, he was again walking away, as he answered.

"That's for me to know, girl. It's two pm. If I were you I'd prepare hard for it." He stated as he exited the room.

I knew Christian would be ruthless and hurt me but as my mind went back to my parents, my ex pack and all those white made me miserable, I held on to the courage of knowing that this would all be worth it.

My eyes shifted to my bed as I turned and tossed through out the night. My mind wasn't settled at all. I had formed so many scenarios of how tomorrow's training would be. Would he chain me and ask me to unchain myself? Would he hit me and tell me to go through it all with no emotion at all? Would he smile as I suffer? Knowing Christian, that wouldn't actually be a surprise. He was just a dark man, someone whose eyes could make even the bravest flee for the hills.

Even though he's a harsh person, whose emotions are just all over the place, I couldn't stop the feeling that he had his own secrets that he was hiding. His scarred face, held a story that I knew I would never find answer to.

Christian is like a puzzle that even I know I can't solve and have to accept that I would never know beyond what he lets me know. Even that night he had screamed his lungs out, his emotions were still well hidden. Some parts of me wanted to help him, to fix him, to find out what made him that cold. What took away the light from his eyes. The light every person has until it's stolen away by the world. Yet, another sane part of me knows it's none of my business and never will it be. For even I, I have my own demons to fight. My own pain to deal with.

And even if I did find out, what would I do? I couldn't even deal with my own pain and sadness.

Dark thought of my past floated back to my mind and I shake my head rapidly as I gave myself hope that some people go through worst than me. Yet, that doesn't mean it hurts any else.

I turn to my alarm clock and I'm beyond shock when I realize it's almost midnight. Turning to my side I block out every other thoughts from my mind and try to find sleep, which by some miracle actually works.

The last thing on my mind is the fact that tomorrow will be nothing but pain.

Chapter 14

I held my ribs and limped away from the training ground. My muscles worn out and every bone and part of me begging me to take rest. Christian had been anything but gentle. His hits, punches had all been so accurate and I had failed miserably. However that couldn't compare to all the times he kept taunting me, throwing harsh and painful words to me. How weak and meaningless I actually was. That tore me, reminding me of all the times I had been weak. All the times I had been stuck in my pack with no one to stick up for me. It made me recall all those memories and my hits on him became sloppy and uncoordinated.

This was Christian's chance and he had fully utilised it. Every bone in me was begging me to surrender. Even my silent wolf, had began to stir and a few whimpers had escaped her. He punched, kicked, ripped and hit every opening in me. I was ready to give up. But I remembered why I was doing this. Why I was willing to go through this and a new determination had formed, and even though at the end, I failed, I was glad, that I was still standing, still willing to fight even with my scars.

Even Christian has slightly out up when he had seen how much I was willing to put my efforts into this. I hissed as the warm water cascaded down my back leaving a burning feeling on all the bruises on my body. I glared at the red spot that currently occupied the left side of my rib. And suddenly my hate for christian grew deeper.

After a struggling for a few hours in the shower, I finally manage to complete and finally step out. I quickly pull on an oversized sweatpants and a black t-shirt that was obviously two times my size.

I had given him freedom to hurt me, to destroy me and just like that, a part of me snapped. I wasn't going to let anyone work over me anymor. I wasn't going to go through the same thing I went through in the past. I was going to stand up for myself. I was going to be a better version of me. And I would die trying.

I limped towards my bed, pain radiating through me. I knew that tomorrow would be even more thorough but I was ready for it. I would push my body until it accepted the challenge. Until I was ready. I refuse to be weak.

I was up by four, took a very light breakfast and already matched to the training ground. The cold air hit my face and it only manages to motivate me. I was already jogging, the air leaving a sweet sensation on my bare arms and legs.

I did not have to wait for long though because I felt him just right behind me. Before I could even react or tell him that I had already heard him, I felt a sharp jab to the side of my ribs. I don't get to recover before another sharp hit is directed to my shoulder blades. He wanted that. He wanted me to notice him so he can get me off guard.

I knew then that my training had began. I had to defend myself somehow.

"Why aren't you defending yourself, Ciane. You know you're weak, right. Your pack abandoned you. Your family left you too. Your parents died because they couldn't stand you! You're weak! Your mate rejected you, right?!" He stated as he continued his assault on my body. The words grated through my heart leaving a very painful sensation.

Pure cold rage pulls me in its grasp and a huge growl escapes my lips. He loves taunting me. He loves seeing me suffer. He did this yesterday and I couldn't fully comprehend the benefit of his brutal abuse to my emotions. He knew how sensitive I was about my past. I had not even told him and he was unconsciously taking it lightly and toying with it.

So, with the cold emotions running through me, I quickly fisted my hand and deliver a quick punch to his stomach. He wasn't fully prepared for it and I managed to get him off guard.

That was the first hit I had ever hit him and I expected a different reaction from him though.

Instead of getting shocked or surprised, he cackles. Instantly my eyes widen in utter bewilderment.

"Just one hit. One hit, Ciane and you're feeling so good about yourself. I am going to break that little confidence you've got going there! Come on then, show me what you got, little girl!" Christian says and my eyes darken in pure rage. A growl leaves my lip so loud it sends spasms of shock through me.

I barrel myself towards him, all my emotions and energy racing through me. I go to punch him but he side step and my rage increases further. I repeat the same process and each time, I miss. I was growing frustrated and my energy was diminishing. He kept hauling harsh words. And suddenly, I stopped.

Rage turns into pain. He was enjoying my suffering and I didn't know how much I could hold on. He was enjoying the pain I was feeling and I wasn't even half way through this training.

"Giving up already?" He taunted and I fall to my knees. I felt so weak and tired. The taunting, the hurt. He wasn't going to stop was he?

"Why? Why are you doing this to me?" I whispered.

"If you meet an enemy right here right now don't you think he'd use any means to destroy you? Don't you think he'd make you vulnerable before taking you out? Life isn't about roses and flowers. If someone emotionally manipulated you, would you start breaking down in the middle of your fight asking the reason for their action? They'll rip your throat out without any hesitation." He explained, his voice cold and detached as usual.

My eyes rise to meet him in confusion.

"So this taunting was all a lesson?" I asked in pure bewilderment. How psychotic is he? "You intentionally said those harsh words to get a reaction out of me?"

"I am teaching you life lessons Ciane and if you're this slow, I don't think we are going to complete this." He muttered angrily. "Do not let your emotions get the best of you. While it gives you rush and energy to take out your opponent, it also makes your moves sloppy and uncoordinated, just as witnessed. Emotionally derived strength is weak and unstable. Let your emotion dictate your actions and you'll be heading to an early grave. Lesson 1 complete. Be here by 4.00 am tomorrow. Tomorrow isn't going to be this easy. I have warned you." He emphasized as he walked away.

Before I could even reply, he was already exiting the room. I sat on the floor for almost ten minutes in shock. I was contemplating my decision right now. What exactly would he do next? Chain me and tell me not to scream while he beat me? I had chosen this ad I knew that only pain would shape me.

I wasn't ready but I was going to give it my best.

Chapter 15

Two weeks had gone by in a blur. Christian was anything but gentle. I had learnt that the hard way the first time his fist had hit me. He lacked emotions and he enjoyed torturing me. I had seen firsthand how sadistic he could be. After he had 'emotionally tortured' me, his training had grown even harder. I was on the verge of giving up most of the time but somehow, somehow I got the strength to keep going.

I also noticed that in those two weeks, my body was becoming more toned, more muscled and I wasn't complaining one bit. It was one of the perks of the vigorous and tormenting training I was going through. The only one actually.

Today however, when I awoke at the right time, Christian was no where to be seen. I was so accustomed to our daily routine that his sudden disappearance was quite odd and left an uncomfortable feeling within me. I barely knew him and wouldn't say I was overly concerned for the guy but I was curious. What could have possibly come up?

Maybe it's another of his crazy 'tests' and I knew I needed to be ready for a thorough session with him. However, an hour later, I knew he wasn't going to show up. I sighed and dropped down on the mat, my legs and arms spread wide apart from each other as I made 'mat angels'

I was already so bored laying on the mat so with a rash decision, which I knew I'd completely regret, I get up and match towards his supposed room. I had ever really gone there after the time I had accidentally seen him crying his eyes out.

I match towards his said room and pushed the door open only to be met with. . .nothing. He wasn't in and it looked like he hadn't been in for an entire night. Maybe he went out? But where?

In the past few months I've been here, he had never gone out. Always doing something or training me. I always tried my best to avoid him at all cost. I did not know what to think of his sudden disappearance and I honestly did not want to know.

I prepare myself some coffee and made a few pancakes for myself. Surprisingly, he had said he didn't mind if I used any of the things and food he had. Of course he did not state it out.

Two days later and he still wasn't back. Each morning I woke up at 4.00am and headed to the training ground. Maybe he got bored and abandoned me in this gigantic house in the middle of nowhere.

It was early morning and I was busy taking my second cup of coffee when a loud noise echoes through the empty house. I ignore it not ready to move away from the comfort of my sit. I try to take a sip only for the same noise to interrupt my mood. I knew I had to go and check. Maybe it's another rogue? That shocks me and I immediately shoot up from my sit, heading towards the door, where the noise was growing quite loud as if someone wanted to get in.

I quietly tiptoed towards the source, my eyes eyeing the bat that was by the couch. Reasons it was there? I didn't know but I was thankful for it. With quick fluid movements, I run over and grab it, clutching it tightly with both my hands. I tip toe towards the door where the same noise was still coming from. I knew I wasn't really trained much but I wouldn't go down without a fight. Without Christian here, I had to fend for myself and realize that I was already a grown woman who needs to fight her own battles.

I knew I had to act quickly before the culprit could sense or smell me. I quickly unlocked the door, ready to deliver a life uttering blow. The bat, however, remains mid air when my eyes focuses on the form of the person outside.

My eyes widen comically as I stared at the being who was currently slumped on the floor, his eyes barely open. His face was black and blue with bruises and bloody gushes all over his now barely clad form. I was beyond shocked. What had happened to him. No words left my mouth as I focused on his now closed eyes, breath coming out shallow and barely there.

What happened to him? Was he attacked? But. . . But he's skilled? Who would have done this to him?

"Christian?" I mutter finally realizing the severity of the situation.

Dropping the bat, I clutch his hands that were already laying motionless on his side. I try to lift him, only for me to fall straight on him. He lets out a groan and I knew I had worsened his injuries. I quickly shoot up, taking a few steps away from him.

"Christian, can you get up?" I almost face palm at the outrageous question. Of course he couldn't get up.

Using the little strength that I had I repeat the same thing and this time, I'm successful. I manage to lift him up, and cooperatively, he slings his arm on my shoulder. I push the door open with my foot and slowly lead him inside.

"Umph" I hiss when we almost tumble down. I could tell he was barely conscious and I was praying hard he did not have any internal injury because there'd be nothing I'd do for him.

He was weighing me down but I pushed myself harder leading him up the stairs, each step harder than the last.

I was almost passing out too when we reached his room. I, as gently as I could, laid him on his bed before heading to his bathroom to look for bandages and anything I could use to treat the wounds littered on both his face, arms and hands.

Who would have done this to him? Didn't he fight back? Whoever did it must have gotten away with more wounds that he did. Or so I hope.

I position myself right next to him before I began tending to his wounds. He didn't make any sound even though I was sure the antiseptic stung a lot. After dressing all his wounds, I had nothing else to do. He now looked like a creepy version of a mummy with almost the entire side of his head wrapped in a white bandage.

I took a step and stared at his form that was too calm for my liking. I closed my eyes praying that he'd get better and not die on me. I honestly don't know where I'd put his body if he died. I barely knew him and I didn't know if some relatives would come looking for him or maybe his pack would feel his death? And his mate? I'd never thought of that. He is a complete mystery to me and I was starting to get very weary of it all.

"What the heck happened to you, Christian?" I mutter to myself, knowing fully well I wouldn't get any answer.

I sighed knowing I'd have to come and check and change his bandages soon, if he doesn't die that is. I leave the room and head to the kitchen to prepare some soup in case he woke up hungry. I knew he wouldn't even care that I prepared food for him but I wasn't going to let him starve to death.

A few hours later, the food was already ready and I was preparing myself a cup of hot chocolate. I was ready to head upstairs when I heard a loud scream coming from Christian's room. Without a second thought, I find myself already running towards the room.

Maybe the person had come back to finish what they started? But I would have heard it?

I quickly push the door open ready to tackle the attacker and protect Christian. However, for the second time in a row, my eyes widen in shock as I stared at him. He had tears rolling down his cheeks in a heavy flow. His eyes were closed shut and I instantly knew he was having a nightmare.

It might not even have been a nightmare for I had experienced it too before. I had had the same reaction too and I was frozen.

I did not know what to do.

"No, please don't do it. Don't hurt them. I will do anything. . ." He pleaded, every word uttered filled with pain and utter misery. The Christian I knew, the tough and ruthless man who had trained me a few weeks back was nowhere to be seen. Here was a broken man, crying his heart out for things and people o did not know and for the first time, I felt empathy for him. He had his own fights, demons chasing him.

I take a step towards him and my legs seems to finally work as I ran towards his bed. I instantly held his hand and when he pulled away, I got closer to him, pulling him to my side in an embrace. A much needed one.

"Christian. . .listen to my voice. None of it is real. None of what you're seeing is real. It's all just a dream." I repeat the phrase over and over again until finally stopped muttering the words. I turned to his face only to see him deep in sleep.

I sighed and slowly pulled away from him and exited the room. I honestly did not like how rude and emotionless he has been but, for once, I almost understood why. I almost understood the urge and need to hide his emotions.

I didn't even know if I wanted to tell him what had unfolded tonight.

But something I was certain of was something had happened to Christian. Something painful and dark.

Chapter 16

Christian had barely woken up last night and by morning, I was already so tired and in need of sleep very urgently. I had stayed up almost the entire night checking his temperature, pulse and changing his bloodied bandages. They were improving greatly. I was almost surprised by this. By morning, his face was almost completely healed. His ribs that were thoroughly bruised looked like they were healing slightly. There was much difference from the dying Christian from last night and the one from this morning who looked very much alive.

A huge yawn left my mouth, reminding me of the fact that I had barely slept last night. I rub my eyes before preparing a much needed cup of coffee. If I didn't take it, I'm pretty sure I'd just fall asleep.

When I'm done, I head back upstairs expecting Christian to still be in bed, only to find an empty bed. Before I could panic, I hear the familiar sound of the shower going on. Of course he had woken up.

I exit the room and head towards the kitchen where I had left the delicious coffee. Taking a sit by the counter, I pour myself another cup and take a huge sip of the hot caffeine and without realizing it, a huge sigh escapes my lips. Delicious.

I was taking the final gulp of my coffee when my eyes connect with those of Christian as he walked down the stairs, his hands holding his ribs. He had on a white t-shirt and some black pants. His hair laid messily on top of his head, still dripping slightly from the shower he just took.

"Hey, how are you feeling?" I ask, my voice sounding too gentle for my liking.

"I'm fine." He grumbles. Of course.

"How's your ribs? Do you need anything to eat? Is anything hurting?" I asked again trying to fully comprehend if he was lying or actually he was actually okay. And from the little time spent with him, I'm pretty sure he doesn't want to look weak in front of anyone.

"I said I'm fine! And I would love a cup of coffee." He demands and walks towards the living room. My eyes follows his movements until he finally flops down on the couch. He instantly hisses and clutches his ribs once more. I almost laugh out loud, quite enjoying his misery. I had just asked nicely and he wasn't even grateful that I helped him. He did not even thank me for treating his wounds, staying awake almost the entire night to take care of him. How typical of him.

"Yeah, if you're feeling that fine, you can come and prepare your own coffee." I glare and decide to go to my room to catch up on some much needed rest.

"Fine, I'm sorry. Can I just have some coffee, please." I almost gape at him. He actually apologized.

"Fine, only because you asked so nicely."

I prepare him a cup, making sure I add a few spoons of sugar. I bet he loves his coffee black with no sugar. Well, it'll have to do.

I grab the mug and hand him the now bittersweet drink. He takes a sip and sighs.

"It's good."

"Oh, I thought you'd prefer it black like your soul." I whisper only to receive a glare from the said man.

Right. Werewolf hearing.

"Very funny." He rolls his eyes taking another sip from his mug.

I sigh wondering if questioning him right now would be a bad idea. I mean we weren't close or anything but at least he owed me an explanation.

"Whatever you want to ask me, go ahead." Christian says, as if he had already read my mind.

"What happened to you out there?" I ask, my voice almost a whisper. He stays mum and when I'm almost sure he wasn't going to respond, he speaks up.

"It really doesn't matter, Ciane. What's done is done." It was the first time he was using my name with no malice or hate in it. I did not know what to think or feel about that.

"Christian, you showed up bruised and beaten up with wounds all over you! How does that not matter!?" I glare at him. He was acting very immature right now. He places the mug, that he was squishing with his hand, on the glass table and glare at it.

"Just ignore it, Ciane. It shouldn't bother or concern you." He sounded almost frustrated.

"How can I ignore it, Christian! You show up bruised, almost dead and you offer me no explanation. You owe me just that." I was getting mad by the minute and I knew if I kept it up I'd say something I'd fully regret.

"It's nothing, okay! Nothing! And forget about it! Don't act like you care! Don't act as if you don't have secrets too!" He yells, his voice booming through the entire house.

It was a secret? I did not know he'd be this triggered.

"Wait, it has something to do with all those nightmares you're getting, right?" I instantly regret asking it.

His face pales and he instantly shoots up from his sit completely disregarding the fact that he almost lost his life and was still healing. I did not comment because I was busy trying to find a way out of the hole I had just dug up for myself.

"Nightmares?" His voice barely audible.

"Umm...." I was in shock myself.

"You know this is the most you've ever spoken to me." I laugh, the laugh sounding very unreal and nervous.

"Don't change the subject, Ciane. What. Do. You. Mean. Nightmares?" He asks, each word detonated, his eyes burning with fury with a hint of. . .fear? No, I read that wrong. He places his hand on my shoulder keeping me in place.

"Christian, it's not a big deal. Just let it go."

"No, I want to know." He glares at me, his eyes sharp and full on furious.

"Fine, you kept muttering in your sleep for someone to stop and not to hurt some people." I whisper, my voice diminishing as I spoke the words.

"No," He murmurs, the hand on my shoulder going stiff and dropping from there. His eyes held nothing. No anger, no fury, no pain or any other emotion. Completely void. And that scares me.

"Christian, it's not a big deal honestly I am not judging you or anything, I promise." I try, wincing when the words sounds very weird and very cliche. What am I suppose to say, honestly.

"Did I say anything else?" It's like he did not hear what I just said. "No?"

"Forget everything you heard, it meant nothing. And I wasn't screaming for anyone. Just don't bring it up. Ever." His voice sounded void of emotions.

My eyes trace the scar on his face. I had never really focused on it that much but now that I'm close to his face, I could easily note that a blunt object had been forcibly used to scar it. Probably silver because it looked very painful. Our scars almost looked identical. While mine was excruciatingly painful, his looked as if the person who did it wanted to make him remember it and the reason it was there. It was at that moment that I realize, I have no idea who Christian really is.

His back story. Where he came from and why he saved me that night from the rogues. Why he did not let me die. I had asked before why he did it and he said it was out of pity but I felt there was something else. . . something he wasn't telling me.

"Christian, I. . ." I don't finish what I was saying because he storms away, not even glancing back at me. I stare at the cup that still had coffee on the table, almost full.

What have I got myself into? I was confused, tired but mostly frustrated. I did not know why I was getting so invested in him. He wasn't worth my time but I couldn't stop the curiosity clawing at me to discover everything about him.

Chapter 17

A few days had gone by and Christian had not talked to me. I was avoiding him and he was doing the same. The only time I ever saw him was when he came to eat the food I made. After that, he would literally storm away to goddess knows where. Our training had come to an unspoken end, or standstill, I honestly did not know. I did not even dare ask because I wasn't sure of how he would react. Maybe he'd yell at me for he had done it a couple of times before.

I scroll through Netflix, that was paid apparently, trying to find a good show to binge watch because there was literally nothing to do. I had already eaten, washed utensils and cleaned part of the house. I finally settle on The Witcher. I had never really heard of the series but it looked kinda interesting since Henry Cavill was the male lead.

Few hours later I was halfway through the fifth episode and I was getting sleepy. I had barely gotten a sleep the previous night after being swamped by nightmares of the past that can't seem to let me go. I, however, did not wake up screaming like how I did in the past. I did not want to alert anyone and by anyone I mean Christian.

I let out a yawn and immediately realize that if I don't get up I'll fall asleep on the couch. I switch off the TV and decide to explore the monstrous house. I had only been to a few basic rooms in this house which are my bedroom, Christian's, the kitchen and the living room.

I walk through the hallway in the direction of my room and began opening random doors. Most were completely blank while the rest had what looked like broken furniture. It wasn't really interesting and I almost instantly got bored.

I was at the end of the hallway and decide to open the last one. It was completely dark but I could vaguely see the outlines of a bed, a nightstand and a lamp. Without even thinking further, I turn on the lights. The said items were there but I had not fully comprehended what was inside the room. My eyes focus on the pictures that were now visible, all scattered in the room. I pick of the pictures and a girl about fourteen or fifteen with thick blonde hair and brown eyes stood in picture with a wide smile spread on her lips. Her eyes radiating pure happiness. I pick a few more and what shocks me even further is in a few of the pictures, Christian stood next to her, an identical smile lighting up his face. His smooth scarless face looked youthful and full of happiness, unlike the Christian I know now.

Without even realizing it, I plop down on the floor and further looked at the other pictures scattered on the floor. Each picture was taken looked beautiful because of all the emotions portrayed on the faces on the images. One of the pictures had Christian standing with his "supposed sister" and two other people who were smiling at the two who looked to be in an argument that did not even look serious. I could easily note that this picture was taken without their knowledge because the emotions looked genuine and full of happiness. I did not even realize a smile was on my lips as I stared at the pictures.

I grab another photo, only for me to drop it almost instantly. No... There's no way! I grab the picture once more, my eyes widening further. It can't be possible. How does he know her? In the picture, Christian stood next to Anabelle, a wide smile on both their faces. Christian's eyes however were focused on Anabelle, shining with both adoration and love. He looked genuinely happy, his emotions fully exposed, not like the Christian I know who I could barely read.

No.

Not Anabelle.

Anabelle, Exus' sister. My ex mate.

One of the people who had tormented and abused me. How did Christian know this monster?

Anabelle looked kind of happy. It still did not take away the evil glint in her eyes. The same eyes that had found pleasure in seeing me suffer, in seeing me squirm in pain, the eyes that had witnessed most of my pain and had been the source of most of it. I did not even realize my hands were shaking as I stared at the picture. I could feel tears gathering in my eyes as I stared at her. Her eyes looked identical with those of her brother and I hated it.

I was about to place the picture down when a hand suddenly grabs my wrist. I was so lost in my thoughts that I did not even realize that Christian was already next to me, and he looked furious.

I knew I had completely messed up because of how his eyes were turning completely dark. Oh no, what have I gotten myself into. I know I am the one who decided to come in here and I am the one who decided to explore this far.

"What are you doing here?" He said, his eyes burning with fury.

"I. . . I was exploring. I am sorry. I did not mean to come here." I murmur, my voice low and barely audible.

"You were exploring and what? Your hands decided to peak through the pictures?" He hissed, his eyes glaring into my own.

"I am sorry. I just..." I did not want to say.

"Get out!" He stated, his voice too calm. Christian was never calm.

I quickly shoot up and raced out of the room. My mind was no longer focused on Christian's anger or the fact that I somehow invaded his privacy. I was focused on the fact that he knew Anabelle. So, maybe he knows Exus. Exus, the guy who had ruined my life. The guy who was supposed to be a loving mate. The guy who was supposed to be an alpha and take care of all his pack members but failed to do it. He ruined my life. Made me hate myself and created a vengeful person. All those times he took pleasure in hurting me.

I blink away the tears that were gathering in my eyes. Exus and Anabelle did not deserve my tears. I had shedded enough tears to last me a lifetime and I wasn't going to do it again. My life had been ruined by those two and I wasn't going to let them get to me again.

Even now that I am miles away from them, they are still here haunting me. I hated it but I couldn't help it.

However, what bothered me most about this situation is the fact that Christian knows Anabelle and I just couldn't understand how.

Chapter 18

A sigh escaped my lips as I snuggled closer to my duvet, fully enjoying the fact that I was actually getting some much needed sleep. Sleep had evaded me the previous night and I was fully utilizing the sudden calm night.

Suddenly, unprepared, cold freezing water comes in contact with my body. A loud yelp leaves my lips as I shoot up from the bed, wondering what exactly happened.

My eyes scan the room and settle on the man who was currently holding an empty bucket. He did this! The audacity!

"How dare you! What's your problem! Have you lost your mind!?!" I raged, shooting eye daggers at his form. He even has the audacity to smirk at me, folding his arms across his chest. He's literally amused by my now dripping flesh.

"You think this is funny!? Why couldn't you just wake me up like a sane person and why am I awake at 4.00am in the morning?" He only stares at me with amusement in his eyes.

"First of all, this is freaking hilarious and secondly, did you forget your training or have you already given up?" He replies, his eyes holding the same amusement I had witnessed. If I wasn't completely livid, I would have been quite shocked that Christian was showing me some type of emotion.

"Don't you remember you stopped showing up yourself! It has been almost a week now and you're talking about training? I think you have a few lose screws." I fumed.

"That's a bit rude but I couldn't really train you while injured, could I? But if you don't want anymore training, you can go back to sleep. I honestly cannot waste my time on a lazy pupil." He says, already walking towards the door.

Lazy?

Lazy pupil!? He really got guts. I'll show him what a lazy pupil looks like.

I grab my slipper and immediately hurl at his retreating figure. I was almost ready to cackle but he ducks before the shoe could make contact with his back.

"You have a terrible aim, and I would help you with that too but I can't force you." He shrugs.

This is so not him. He has never walked into my room before. He has never willingly helped me out.

"Why are you so willing to help me now when I literally had to beg you the first time?" I asked.

"Well, I don't break my promise and furthermore, you owe me a favour and that's more important than anything. This isn't about you, Ciane, don't even let it cross your mind." Of course it's not about me.

"Yeah but why would you pour freezing cold water on me. Why not wake me up like a normal person?"

"Yeah, where is the fun in that and I was dying to see your reaction." He chuckles before quickly exiting the room. This man is actually finding humor in my misery. But this Christian looked kind of jovial. Almost happy about something. Christian and happiness is equal to disaster and pain for me.

Ten minutes later and I was already standing at the training ground, patiently waiting for Christian who was no where to be seen. He had forced me out of bed only for him not to show up.

I swallow the rage that was bubbling in my stomach, taking deep breaths in order not to murder the said man. I knew though not to let my guard down because knowing Christian, he could easily attack me from behind and call it "training."

I hear his footsteps, before his barely there scent wafted towards me. His scent was also the reason why I could never really tell where he was sometimes and that itself was a mystery to me.

I turn around, ready to defend myself if need be, however when I do, my eyes meet the two mugs he was currently holding in both of his hands. I raise a brow in question.

"What is that?" I ask, my eyes scanning the two mugs in disdain.

"Coffee." He says.

"Coffee?" I ask.

"That's what I just said."

"Why?"

"Why not?"

"But why?"

"But why not?" Seriously.

"Christian, why are you bringing me coffee? You've never done that before?" I ask, almost in disbelief. Why was he doing this today? Why is he so happy.

"Oh, that's right. I can understand why you don't want to trust me. I've never really given you a reason to trust me and for that I'm sorry. I just thought you'd like some. . .what shall I call it...peace coffee?" He explained. He was apologizing.

"Why now? Why are you apologizing now?" I questioned as I eyed the mug that had a very dark liquid. Too dark if you asked me.

"I. . . I don't know. Maybe it's because you took care of me when I was injured. I don't know when but I don't want to be mean to you anymore." He said, almost remorseful.

Really? But why didn't I believe his words. Maybe he's actually having a change of heart? I really truly wanted to believe that but something was holding me back and knowing Christian, he always has a plan. Something up his sleeves. Not fully trusting his words I nod.

"Okay, I know you don't trust me but I'm giving you a choice to choose the mug you want." He said. Wow, whatever plan he has must be big. I decide to go with the flow.

"Fine," I pick the light blue mug, with the liquid half filled. The other mug was full so I completely avoided it. Christian picks up the other mug, and sends me a smile. Okay, very creepy.

"Cheers," he say raising his mug towards mine. I do the same and clink our mugs.

I hesitantly bring the cup closer to my mouth. I sniff the "coffee" wondering about the unique flowery scent emitting from the coffee. Hesitantly, I tip the liquid into my mouth, pouring just a little, only to spit it out almost instantly. The concentration of the "coffee" nearly burning off my tongue. He had really outdone himself this time.

"Really Christian? Wolfsbane?" I wasn't even at all surprised. He took a long sip of his drink, taking almost half of the "coffee"

"Well, I almost succeeded." He whispered.

"That could have killed me!" I hiss pouring the liquid on the floor, now detecting the slight glittery dark powder at the bottom of the mug.

"No, it wouldn't have." He said, almost sure of it.

"And how do you know this, oh wise one?" I glare, keeping the eye roll barely at bay. He did not even seem to care that I would have consumed the entire thing. No wonder he had been so quacky and almost happy.

"Ciane, I have barely talked to you in the past few months you've been here. You have no idea who I am, what I do or where I come from. I am not to be trusted, but yet again I saved you so I deserve the benefit of the doubt. Also, I have been giving you complicated lessons, and each lesson comes in ways you cannot anticipate, making you weary of this little stunt I pulled. My little speech was to make you sympathize with me, giving me the advantage. Your emotions. So because you do not know how to really feel, whether you should trust me or not, you decide to pick the mug with little coffee, in doing so, picking the mug with the higher concentration of wolfsbane. And because you don't know if you can trust me, you'd only take almost a little of the coffee-wolfsbane solution."

I gape at him. He deduced me in a matter of seconds. But who in their right mind would actually trust Christian. He's a walking ticking time bomb.

"Enemies would use any means to make you vulnerable or kill you. If I was someone who wanted you dead, would you still be alive?" He almost raised a brow.

"Wolfsbane, as you know, is horrible to wolves and can kill your wolf instantly if consumed in large concentration. However, in order to lessen the effects of wolfsbane in your system, each morning for this week, you are to mix your coffee with half a tablespoon wolfsbane and in the next week, you'll increase it to a tablespoon until it's effects are dulled in your body. " He said, walking away leaving me to gape at his retreating figure.

Chapter 19

I t had been two whole months and I had no idea how it had just gone by. With the vigorous training and Christian being Christian, I had not even noticed how much time had gone by. Day after day, I was getting used to the early rising and the wolfsbane. I was finally at a 1½ teaspoons. The burn had also lessen from the first time I willingly consumed the harmful liquid. Even Christian had started using wolfsbane coated weapons to see if I was actually taking it, which although it hurt, it was much less compared to when I was in my pack.

In those two months, he did not bring up anything about the pictures I saw. We had been busy and I didn't ask him because I was afraid he'd burst out in anger. I was dying to ask how he knows Anabelle, but I refrained from doing so. However, my restrain was wearing thin and soon, I knew I'd succumb and ask him but until then, I would try and much as I can to avoid the question.

"Concentrate, Ciane!" Christian's yelling snaps me out of my thoughts and I realize he had already raised the crossbow. I duck and an arrow goes zooming above my head.

"A crossbow! Really?! Do you want to kill me?" Knowing him, he wouldn't even care if I get hit or die.

"Jeez, you're becoming a professional drama queen." He rolls his eyes.

I gape at him. That's the most normal thing he had ever said to me in forever.

"Wow, so how am I supposed to dodge an arrow? I'm not the flash."

His brows furrow.

"Who?"

"Never mind but why are you shooting arrows at me?"

"This will enhance your speed and your hearing. A werewolf's hearing is very enhanced so with it you can be able to hear when I shoot, the arrow zooming through the air, if you concentrate." He explains, not even once yelling.

He must like me now. I almost snort.

"So, what and how am I supposed to enhance my hearing?"

"A blind person's senses are more enhanced due to their lack of vision. Their sense of taste, smell and hearing are more enhanced compared to a person who can see."

"So you're suggesting you blind me?" I ask, horror clouding my face. He can't possibly mean that?

"Seriously? Why don't you just let me complete what I'm telling you before rushing into your own unnecessary conclusions?" Christian rages, his glare shutting me up instantly.

"No, I am not going to make you blind. I'm going to blind fold you. As a werewolf, your senses are already enhanced and with temporary removal of one of your senses, you'll have to concentrate on your most important one: hearing." He explains as he walks over to me, pulling a piece of black fabric from the back pocket of his dark jeans.

He walks behind me before wrapping the piece of cloth around my eyes, blinding me.

"Now concentrate. Feel every noise around you, every movement, every small sound."

"Please, don't kill me with that thing." I plead.

I take in a huge gulp of oxygen and followed what he asked of me.

I could hear alot of noises from where I stood. Because we were already deep in the forest, I could hear the chirping of a few birds, the loud crickets, the sound of flowing water dripping down a rock and I could hear a heartbeat. Someone very close to me.

I hear him take a small gasp of air before breathing it out. I hear him grasp something. It sounded very loud. I hear him pull the trigger with a click sound and I hear as the arrow leaves the bow, and almost instantly I duck again as I hear and feel the arrow zoom through the air.

I quickly pull the blind fold off. I turn around and stare at the arrow embedded on the tree. I did it!

"I did it! I did it!" I squealed in joy.

It always takes about 20 times of repetition from Christian so I could finally get it but I did it.

"Yeah, good job." Christian whispers, the corner of his lips curling slightly in a restrained smile or smirk I couldn't tell. It was enough for me though.

"I am becoming a pro at this. I can actually beat you." I smile widely.

"Yeah, whatever. Don't let it get to your head." He grumbles his gaze falling on me, but I could tell he was amused by it all.

I chuckle lightly staring at him.

The questions that have been running through my mind almost flows through my lips at that moment but I manage to ask a simple one.

"Christian, can I ask you something?" I ask, my eyes fixated on his face, waiting for his expression to change.

"If you want to borrow more weapons, then yes knock yourself out." He replies.

"No, not that."

"Okay, go ahead." He states, his brows slightly furrowing in confusion.

I took in a deep breath, my eyes unconsciously straying away from his.

"How do you know Anabelle?" I whisper but I knew he heard me clearly.

I could instantly feel the shift in the air, as he stiffen, his entire body going rigid even though my eyes were not on him.

"What?" He almost growls.

"How-" His loud growl deters me from repeating the question.

"I heard you the first time. How do you know her." His voice sounded both calm and enraged at the same time.

"I...I" I fumble, not knowing what to tell him. Before I could react he was already right in front of me, his face cold, detached and ruthless. He quickly holds my hand tightly, eyes falling on mine.

"How do you know her." It almost came out as a whisper but it sounded so angry.

"I can't tell you." Was the only thing I could come up with.

"Did she send you here? Are you her spy or something?" He asks, his eyes flashing black, showing the raging wolf within him.

However, I was shocked. Her spy?

"What are you going on about? Her spy?" I almost chuckle at how ridiculous he sounded.

"How do you know her?" His hands rising to grab both my wrist in a tight hold.

He looks mad, enraged but there was something else there, desperation. Desperation for what? I couldn't tell.

"Why do you want to know?" I ask back.

"Ciane, answer my question now!" He screams at me and my own rage simmers through me.

"No! You cannot do this to me again! I patched you up when you showed up bruised and broken and you refused to tell me what happened to you then, and now! Now you're demanding answers from me when I was the one who asked you the question! At least give me one answer for goddess's sake!" I rage as I pull myself away from him, my fist clenched so tightly, I could feel my claws digging into my palm.

His eyes had already turned completely dark and I stood waiting for him to snap my neck. His hand were clenched so tightly that if I did not dare move a muscle.

I was mad, angry at him. He was demanding answers from me when he himself wasn't willing to give me his. Even just one. I know it sounds wrong to demand answers from him but he wasn't willing to tell me anything at all and I was anxious for them.

I was ready to walk away from him and never talk to him ever again when he finally replied, the answer still shocking even though I had almost expected it.

"She was my mate."

He did not even wait for my reaction before storming away, his shoulders stiff.

I glare at the spot he was a few seconds ago, almost feeling guilty for pressing him for answers.

Key word being almost.

Chapter 20

He was avoiding me like the plague and whenever we made eye contact, he'd almost instantly avert his eyes or completely exit the room. He had told me apart of his life really and I wanted to just share with him a sliver of mine. He was however nowhere to be seen.

I sighed as I added wolfsbane to the coffee I was drinking. The bitter liquid turning even more bitter if not utterly painful to consume. I was growing used to it though and I ignored the feeling of it flowing down my throat.

I was about to take another sip when Christian's heavy footsteps echoes right behind me. I quickly shuffle and turned to stare at him. He only quickly glanced at me before and walked towards the stairs.

"Christian, can we talk?"

He was quiet for a few seconds before walking towards me and plopping down on the sit right next to me. I did not want to begin the conversation and luckily I did not have to.

"I'm sorry," My eyes widen.

"What?" I mutter, utterly shocked.

"Don't make me repeat it." He sighs.

"Why?" I ask perplexed, eyes focusing on him.

"Forcing answers out of you while I did not even explain myself to you." He sighs.

"Who are you an what have you done to Christian?" I ask, my eyes still wide open, gaping at him.

"Yeah yeah whatever but honestly, you were there to nurse my wounds when no one was and that's quite alright of you. I should have thanked you then." He grumbles, looking very uncomfortable making me realize it's not something he does so often.

I guess he forgot the fact that it's only the two of us in this forsaken mansion in the middle of nowhere. And if he was to die, I'd be on my own. I kept the thought to myself.

"Why now? What changed?" I ask, cautious of this suddenly nice Christian.

"Wait, is this another one of your mind games because if it is, then I'm done." I state, getting quite mad.

"No it's not." He glares, going quiet for a few seconds before continuing, "I don't trust you too, if that eases your worries." Really? No it doesn't. I glare at him.

"Okay, that's rude." I state, staring at him, my face blank.

"What am I supposed to say then?" He grumbles.

"The apology will do."

"Okay," he says staring at me expectantly.

"What?"

"What did you want to talk to me about?" He asks.

I realized at that moment he's speaking more words to me recently than he has for the last couple of months I've been here.

"Oh, right. Since I practically forced you to tell me who Anabelle is to you, I wanted to tell you how I know her." I say, my eyes on him.

"You don't have to, really." This isn't Christian. What happened to the heartless guy?

"Are you sure you're okay?" I grumbled, my eyes scanning his face that looked identical to Christian's, only the personality doesn't match.

"Ciane, you can either go on with it, or leave me alone." He snarls, getting mad. Jeez. Bipolar much.

"No need to get mad for nothing." I sighed, my eyes leaving his face, "I know her because she is my ex mate sister." I whisper, rather very softly.

I don't see or note his reaction. There's only silence.

My eyes fall on him but his eyes had glazed over.

"Christian, what is wrong?" I whisper.

"But that would make you Exus' mate? How?" He states.

Of course he knows my ex mate. The man who was responsible for the my tears and years of pure torment.

"You know Exus?" That question sounded stupid even to my own ears. There's no way he'd not know Exus.

His fist clench tightly on his sides, eyes glaring at the carpeted floor with so much rage and hate in them. He gives me a subtle nod that I almost miss.

"What happened?" I was pushing my luck but the more he answered my questions, the more curious I became. He was mad, I could tell from the claws that were already digging deeply into his flesh.

"You don't need to answer if you don't want to Christian. If it's making you uncomfortable, you don't have to." I explain, and he lets out a breath of air, his fist unclenching. He did not want to talk about it and I understood because I also did not want to speak myself. I know he knew that something pretty bad happened in the past to me and I know he has a pretty good idea who it involves.

Silence rings out in the living room, both of us deep in our own thoughts when suddenly a thought goes through my mind.

"You would be my brother-in-law." I state quietly.

A small chuckle escapes his mouth as his eyes lightly light up with humor. His soulless dark eyes looked rather enchanting at that quick second and I couldn't help appreciate his face. Even with the scar that occupied the left side of his face, he looked handsome.

Hold up! Nope! Never go there!

I reprimand myself as I quickly look away from him. He doesn't respond so I continue, as if talking to myself.

"I wonder how that would have been." I wonder out loud, trying to imagine a cold emotionless Christian as my brother-in-law. It did not suit him.

We fall into silence once again not knowing exactly what to talk about after avoiding each other for almost an entire year now. Christian had been focused on training me and being mean and I did the same while trying to avoid Christian.

"Okay, this is weird. I've never pictured us sitting together talking you know." I chuckle, the sound leaving my lips, nervous and before he can reply I continue, "Maybe, we can finally be friends?" I say.

I was really pushing it today and knowing Christian he could actually easily reject the whole idea and walk away. However, I don't regret the question.

"Friends?" He raises a brow.

"Yeah, friends." I raise my hand for him to shake it.

He hesitantly lifts his and places in mine. It was the first time we were holding my hand willingly, all the other times being forced contacts between the two of us.

I firmly shake it, a small smile slipping to my lips. I glance up at his face and a small one, barely there lit up his. He looked less harsh and more human than I have ever seen him. The dark shadow always clouding him less visible.

"So what should we do now as friends?" He asks, emphasizing on 'friends' before letting go of my hand.

"We should spar now that we are friends." I reply, my eyes falling on him.

"That's a good idea." He shoots up from his sit and began walking towards the small training field.

I follow my new "friend", feeling my heart warm for the first time in what feels like forever.

Chapter 21

"You're good at this now." Christian complimented as I left the training field, him in tow.

Being friends with him had proved to be really beneficial because I could actually bring it up everytime we sparred or any time I felt like getting something from him, which wasn't much but was worth it. I could tell it was starting to irritate him very much.

"Why thankyou, friend." I give him a toothy smile.

"Why did I agree to this friendship thing." He grumbles rubbing his forehead.

"Hey, no need to be so mad about it." I roll my eyes, glaring at him.

"So, what should we do?" I smile.

"What do you want to do?"

"Maybe we should watch a movie."

"No." He grits, his eyes growing cold.

"Why not?" I glare, folding my arms across my chest.

"I'm not going to sit with you and watch some romantic movies." He growls.

"Jeez, bold of you to assume we were going to watch romance." I roll my eyes once again. "We are going to watch horror, now come on."

"Which one?" He mumbles, trailing behind me, his voice barely even audible.

"Texas Chainsaw massacre." I murmur. I had watched it a while back and it was just very creepy to be honest.

"That's not scary."

I gape at him.

"Of course you'd say that. Your life itself is a real life horror." I point out and receive a heated glare from the man.

He grunts as we walk into the house.

Many minutes later I was glaring at the tv trying to make all the gory details disappear. I hate horror movies, I realize too late.

A squeal escapes my lips when the raving chainsaw roars in the room.

"Stop screaming." Christian grunts shooting me a disappointed look.

"Why aren't you scared or even reacting to this?" I glare.

"Because it's not scary." His voice neutral and bare of any emotion, "Now shut up."

"Jeez," I mumble, sighing and shutting my eyes off for a second and regretting it instantly when I open them and cringe when I see someone's head detach from their body.

Two hours later, I'm already shivering, glaring at Christian who has a smug and an amused expression on his face.

"I though you loved horror movies." His lips tilt up barely as he stares at me, his jagged scar making him more appealing for some reason.

"I did not say I love horror movies." I grumble, evading my eyes from his.

"Okay whatever." He murmurs walking away from me.

"Wait, where are you going?" I ask my eyes following his form.

"Away from you."

"But we're friends now. You're not supposed to just ignore your friends when they want to spend time with you." I explain and he halts. I hear him let out a curse and a sigh escapes his lips.

"What now? Wasn't the movie enough for you, friend?" He grits.

Confidently, I answer him without any hesitation, "No, I still want to know you,"

"What do you want now?" He looked rather irritated as he walked back towards me.

"Let's play 20 questions." I expected him to stare at me blankly and ask what that means instead he sighs and walks over back to the couch.

"And if there's a question you don't feel comfortable answering you can just say "pass" or something." I mumble, occupying the spot next to him.

"Get on with it,"

"Okay, so what's your full name?"

"Christian Blake Knight."

He stays quite. I raise a brow and he stares at me in confusion.

"Dude, it's your turn to ask me a question." I explain and he sighs. I can tell I'm forcing all these on him.

"What's your full name?"

"Glad you asked, I'm Ciane Holden."

"Your middle name?"

"It's my turn." Not telling anyone my middle name.

"Where do you get all the food supply and all other things in this mansion in the middle of nowhere."

"Sometimes it's delivered or I buy everything. Usually I go out on a Saturday."

"How do you get there and why don't I see you leave?"

"There's a mall a few miles from here and we didn't talk before this." He grumbles, looking rather bored.

"When's your birthday?" He asks.

"20th November." I smile.

"Okay, my turn. What's your favorite color?"

It's black like his soul.

"Green."

"Wow, thought you'd say black you know-"

"Like my soul, I get it." Christian grumbles as he rolls his eyes and I gape at him. He rolled his eyes.

We stay quite for a while. My eyes meet his and for the first time, they don't look cold, emotionless or empty. The eyes I am so used to. I could feel him studying my face, his eyes trailing the scar almost identical to his that occupy the side of my face. I always felt it looked rather disgusting back then but now, I was starting to love it honestly. It shows how strong I actually am. I already knew his question before he even asked though and I don't know if I was ready to explain it or even tell him.

"How did you get the scar?" His voice came out as a whisper.

All at once, they come back. All the times Exus hit me, tortured me for his own sick twisted pleasure, the time he let his sister do the same. All the time he ridiculed me, called me names, hurt me, beat me up. I could vividly recall as he carved my face with a silver knife, knowing full well it would not heal no matter what. And in a twisted way, he turned out to be my mate. A mate I had never really truly desired but couldn't avoid. I avert my eyes from his glaring at the marble table.

"You don't have to answer it." His voice snaps me back to reality and I quick sigh leaves my lips.

"Exus."

"Why?" He asks, almost instantly.

Why is a good question. Why though? Why had Exus found pleasure in hurting me, in making me suffer. I could not understand why and I never bothered to know.

"No, it's my turn now," I smirk,

"Fine."

"Which pack are you from?" I ask.

His eyes however turn dark at the mention of that. I could see his fist clench tightly, a distant look flooding his eyes. I didn't think the mention of his pack would make him mad. I couldn't comprehend how or why. It didn't make sense. Maybe he is a rogue?

"You don't have to answer if you don't want to." I remind him.

"No." He says, his eyes looking empty, haunted and just some how full of raw pain. He however, continues even though he didn't look willing or ready to talk. "My pack is Night Star Pack."

It took only a second for what he said to register in my brain.

No. It cannot be true. That isn't right.

It couldn't be though. How was that possible?

I stare, wondering if he's actually joking. How could it be. I couldn't understand how.

Chapter 22

"Alpha, Anne is here concerning her transfer to Shadow Stone Pack. Should I let her in?" Jonah, my beta inquires as he stares at me, the caution very evident in his eyes. The look completely understandable.

The past few months to say I've been mad would be an understatement. I have completely destroyed my office too many times and all because I could not stop thinking of her. The woman who was supposed to be my world and I had let slip through my fingers. The woman I had broken almost beyond repair. I had hurt her so badly, my actions unredeemable.

My once lavender scented clean office now reeks of alcohol that I've consumed over the past months. There was no one to blame but myself. Everything that have occured in the past few months completely my fault.

I could not stand the sight of people, of my pack members especially mates. Mine was out there and I couldn't tell if she's okay or not, hurt or not. Was she even still alive? I quickly shut the thought out. She can't be dead. I would have felt the snap, the emptiness that comes with the death of ones mate. Nonetheless, I could feel the emptiness, and it felt she was barely there. Some days, I could feel her, other times I felt empty and the empty days were growing longer.

The sight of Jonah manages to create a burning fury at the pit of my stomach. I quickly drag the lower drawer of my office desk open and pull a bottle of whiskey. I pour a large amount of the content into my mouth, grimacing slightly at the burn as the liquid flows down my throat and I savor the feeling.

"Alpha?" Jonah's voice shatters the little blissful moment and I send him a harsh glare.

"Jonah, leave me alone." I state calmly. Too calmly. Jonah couldn't take the hint. I could feel the familiar sprouting of fur on my skin and I knew what would happen if he didn't leave.

"But, this is the fourth time this week she has come requesting a transfer. Her ma-"

Before he could react I was already up and grabbing him by his neck. His eyes widen when they meet mine that had already turned black. I press even harder on his throat, cutting off his breathing and he began to squirm trying to leave my grasp, which is futile.

"How many times am I supposed to tell you to get out!" I tighten my hold on his neck and I could see him struggling for air.

"I don't care what your demands are when I tell you to get out! You get the f- out of my office!" My voice echoes through the office.

His eyes begin to roll back and I let him go knowing he'd pass out soon.

"Now get out!"

"Ye..yes alpha." His voice almost completely gone as he rushes out of the office.

I flop down on my swivel chair, a sigh leaving my lips. I had done that to one of my pack member. I couldn't understand how things had completely gone wrong. Ever since she left, every little control I had disappeared. Yet, all of it was my fault.

I've always had anger issues but it was quite manageable back then, now I was a ticking time bomb waiting to explode any second now. The pack was noticing my slip ups, my anger and soon, the elders would and I would have to step down as alpha. I can't let that happen. She must come back, whatever it takes.

The door to my office slams open again and I was about to yell some even more colorful words to the intruder but they die in my throat when my eyes meets with my sister's as she walks in.

"Jeez this place smells worse each day." She comments pinching her nose, her face scrunching up in disgust.

"What did you do to your poor beta. He looked ready to pass out any second." She continues, her eyes running through the now dirty and disgusting office.

"Anabelle, leave me alone!" The sight of her irks me even further.

"Are you still mourning that stupid she wolf again? Aren't you tired of drinking and completely doing nothing? Exus, you're a grown man, act like it." She sighs glaring at me, disappointed.

"She's not just some she wolf, she's my mate and could you just leave me be!" I almost scream. She should really do it.

"Yeah yeah, I've heard that over and over. It's time you stopped acting like a complete idiot and move on. How long has it been? A whole year?." She grumbles as she folds her arms across her chest.

"Just leave me alone!" I finally snap, as I go to pour more liquor into my mouth and realize it's empty. I was barely drunk and I pull the other drawer taking out the whiskey mixed with wolfsbane to make my kind drunk. I unscrew the cap and pour a generous amount of it into my mouth, feeling the sting on my tongue but enjoying it nonetheless.

"Dude, you're so messed up." Anabelle says, as she stares at the bottle in my hand.

I could almost instantly feel the effect of it in my body.

Anabelle stays quite for a few seconds and I was about to ask why she was here. Anabelle and I have never had a good relationship. Not that we even tried to get close. And whenever she even shows up it is to complain about or demand for something. Which is utterly ridiculous and annoying.

"What do you really want, Anabelle? I know you're not here to check on me." I glare at her as I take another gulp out of the bottle.

"You're right brother, as always." She chuckles, the dark sound manages to send a shiver down my spine. She can be really creepy at times.

"Do you still visit the bitch." The question enrages me slightly and unconsciously a snarl leaves my lips.

"Not for the past few months, no."

"Are you sure she's even still alive?" Anabelle asks, her green eyes identical to mine, stare into my soul. They look dead.

"I don't know Anabelle. As you can see I have no time for that. I'm sure there are guards guarding the cells. They won't let her die." I explain, rolling my eyes in the process.

"Why are you curious anyway. You were the one who demanded we put her in the darkest part of our prison, remember." I remind her, the slight slur in my words quite prominent. "You remember what she did, right?"

Her face scrunch in confusion before going blank, "Yes, I remember."

Does she really?

"I will go check on her if that makes you feel better." I slur the words and almost roll my eyes at how sentimental that sounded.

"Careful brother, it almost sounds like you care." She shoots me a smirk as she exits my office.

I loved my sister even though I hardly showed that side to her but I know she knows that I do.

I stumble out of my chair, the alcohol finally numbing every emotions that have been so desperate to block out. It however could not block away the face of my mate. The mate I had broken and used, abused and humiliated over and over again.

My mind could never erase that specific moment I discovered she was my mate and the events before all that. I could remember vividly as I pressed my lips on hers, not caring about the consequences of my deeds because then, she was a nobody, someone of no consequence, I could use and dispose. I remember seeing her in the kitchen as she gathered what looked like food. I should have guessed it then, I should have seen the signs that she was about to run away. I should even have paid attention to the sweet scent that had wafted itself to my nose but I was so caught up in trying to press the knife to her shoulder for hurting me. I was the one that hurt her. I was the one that tore her apart and the moment the knife had embedded itself on her shoulder, she turned around.

And my eyes met hers. I knew then I would never really have her. I would never be the one for her for how could I be when I had inflicted most of the pain on her. I had been the source of her hurt. I could feel the tears gathering in my eyes for the millionth time.

Whoever said alcohol numbs feelings lied because all the rage, pain and regret I feel is elevated and somehow I love the feeling because it tortures me. It tortures me to remember all the times I hurt her. All the times I broke her. And that I could never really get her back.

I staggered, heading towards the cells my arms and legs flailing, almost failing to keep me upright. She was there. A few guards by the door send me concerned looks before bowing slightly and letting me pass through. I walk further down and take a flight of stairs to the underground cells where she is. I could not tell if she was alive or not. The place reeked of sweat, blood and urine, it being the worst dungeon in Wolf Creek Pack.

I walk in further, stumbling in the process until I was right outside her cell. I stare at her, my blurry eyes taking in how thin and un-healthy she looks. She deserves it for what she did to my sister.

Her skin that was once tan looked dirty and pale, her once blonde hair brown and matted. The blue jeans and black shirt look big from the loss of weight. The dark eyes identical to those of her brother stares at me with pure hate and malice. They look so cold and empty.

"Exus." Her voice hoarse sounded empty lacking emotions.

"Olivia."

"What do you want now? Isn't my imprisonment enough for you? Are you here to kill me finally?" She doesn't even look worried. Instead rather bored.

"You know what you did to my sister." I slur out the words, almost tumbling to the floor.

"Please enlighten me once again Exus, what exactly I did to your whore of a sister?"

A growl escapes my lips as I grasp the metal bars only to instantly let them go when they sting my hands. Oh right, the silver.

"Do not call her that!"

"Soon, you and your pack will pay for what you did to mine," Olivia says with such conviction, I almost actually believe her.

"You don't get to play the victim here!" The words instantly leaves my lips, although terribly slurred.

"Get your facts right, Exus because every decision you've ever made will soon have it's consequence." She goes quiet, after that and curls up in the corner, her back facing me.

Through the rips and tears in her shirt, I could see the whips marks and scars littered all across her skin from all the torture she has suffered at my hands and my pack warriors.

"I heard your mate left you. She deserves better if you ask me." They came out so hushed that I could barely hear them.

Cold burning rage rushes through my veins and almost instantly dies out when I realize she's correct. I don't deserve her. I never have and never will.

I quietly leave the cell, Olivia's words replaying in my head. My actions? What facts?! They deserve it! They deserve everything for what they did!

Chapter 23

I was fifteen.

Fifteen when Night Star Pack was brought to the ground. Demolished. Many members of the pack were killed and I heard the few that survived fled. I never knew how it happened and did not bother. I empathized with the pack but couldn't do anything for the I was in my own hell.

Night Star Pack was among the strongest packs and for it to crush and burn almost in an instant was shocking. I recall almost vividly that a week before the pack's demise, Exus and his sister who were already barely there at the pack, disappeared and when he showed up, his anger had doubled, his eyes cold and barely containing any emotion. I remember the beating, the crude words, the scars that embedded themselves to my skin and soul. It was one of the worst times of my life and try as I might, the memories would never leave me.

Yet, at this moment I couldn't understand how Christian belonged to a pack that was annihilated five years ago. A pack that has barely crossed my mind since then.

"How is that possible?" My voice is barely audible as I ask the question.

"I was among the few survivors." He said, and I could almost feel the raw pain from those few words.

"I'm so sorry." It's the only thing I could offer him at that moment.

"Yeah, it is what it is." He murmurs before getting up and walking away. I did not know what to say to make the situation better.

I couldn't even try to understand how he feels. Losing ones pack must hurt so much especially if most of the pack members die. I sigh and head to my room. It quite sad to think of the fact that I don't have anything to do or anyone else to talk to. I don't have a phone and I have zero friends. Never had any in the pack and now it's just me and Christian.

Even though I don't want to admit it, he's my first friend. I could never seem to make friends, no matter how much I tried, how much I tried to fit in in the pack, it was just never enough and when my parents died, Exus noticed me. Noticed a vessel he could take his anger out on. I groan rubbing my forehead as I open the door to my room.

I slam the door to and fall face first on the bed, trying to keep the thoughts of that man at bay. That man who keeps plaguing my mind for all the wrong reasons. And I thought wolves were supposed to love their mates regardless of their actions. If they are horrible or not to them. Yet, the only emotion I feel for him is hot burning rage and hate. Hate for all the times he hurt me, all the smug looks he would give me after a thorough beating, all the times he'd let his sister join in the fun.

I roll over and shut my eyes trying to shut my mind too. Shut all the memories of them too. Unconsciously, my mind drift to Christian. I could now understand the reason for his cold and detached behavior. For his barely readable expressions. The need to hide for if he revealed his emotions, it'll only portray the pain, hurt and agony he feels within. There's a lot I don't know about him but for the first time, I understand him.

I don't know how long I get lost in my thoughts but a loud knock from the door snaps me from the crude thoughts. I glance to the window and realize it's already dark. I did not even notice the time. My eyes focus back to the door. The only other person here with me is Christian but I couldn't help but cautiously walk to the door and pulled it open, preparing for a fight.

My eyes widen when I take in Christian who is slightly hunched back, his eyes quite red, a bottle in hand, strong smell of liquor and wolfsbane flowing from him.

"Christian?" I question very confused by his behavior. I have never seen him consume alcohol. I did not even think he had them at all.

"Ciane," he slurs the word out and takes a step forward only for him to stumble and almost falls to the floor. I'm quick enough to stabilize him before he crashes down.

"Oh goddess, you're actually drunk." I whisper to myself as he chugs down the alcohol once more like water.

"Christian, stop it!" I try to pull the bottle from his hand, only he's not willing to part with it.

"Ciane let me just drink, please." He begs, although the words are very slurry, almost impossible to understand. He's begging?

"Why are you drinking anyway, Christian?" I sigh and let him be leaving the bottle in his grasp.

"I just want to forget." He whispers, the emotions from earlier surfacing.

I did not want to question him while drunk but I couldn't leave him all alone with his thoughts. It would eat me up.

"Come," I lead him to the small couch in my room.

"I'm sorry about everything, Christian." I whisper when I finally place him on the couch. I occupy the spot next to him and keep my eyes on him.

"I just...just miss them." He stutters and drops the now empty liquor bottle on the floor.

"I know." I didn't but I did not want to question him.

"They were killed right in front of me and I couldn't do anything. Nothing." He slurs, resting his head on the couch. I don't know what to tell him to assure him that it's okay so I remain quiet as I listen.

"My sister, they took her too from me. I couldn't even save her. I tried, I really did but I couldn't. It wasn't my fault. It wasn't! It wasn't!" He repeats it over and over, almost trying to convince himself that it's true, "It wasn't my fault, right Ciane?" He asks suddenly looking frantic as he grasps my hands in his, his eyes begging me to agree.

Even though I don't know what fully happened but I'm certain that he wouldn't let his family go so easily. He wouldn't let them get hurt or let anything bad happen to them. That I am sure of.

"No it wasn't Christian, it wasn't your fault." I reply my answer genuine.

"You promise?" His eyes looked innocent and youthful and I couldn't help the smile that tug at my lips.

"I promise, Christian."

His eyes search mine and when he's satisfied, a wide grin spread through his lips and I'm in awe. I have never seen him fully smile and to say he looks gorgeous would be understatement.

His eyes stare into mine for a while, longer than comfortable and I look away. I suddenly feel his fingers on my chin as he tilts my face towards his. His black eyes looked happy at that moment. It also held another emotions I couldn't quite decipher. My eyes glue to his in a heated moment.

What is he doing?

"You're really beautiful." He whispers and my eyes widen beyond belief. Christian is complimenting me? I almost laugh. However, I couldn't help the blood that rushes to my cheeks. No one had ever called me that before, just my parents.

"Uh. . .thanks." I stutter, not knowing what to think of the bizarre situation.

"Exus was an idiot to let you go." His words although heavily slurred, sounds genuine and that makes my heart race a bit faster. I pull away from his hand and stare at his red eyes.

How many bottles of alcohol did he consume because normal Christian would never say such words. Not that I'm not enjoying it.

"How many of those bottles did you take?" I ask eyeing him warily.

"About 23, I did not count." He slurs.

"That's quite a few bottles for you to be this drunk."

"Well, they contain wolfsbane and wolfsbane doesn't really do the job anymore." He confesses and I just gape. Twenty three bottles of liquor mixed with wolfsbane?

"Well, let's get you to your room so you can sleep it off." I get up but he shakes his head.

"Can... Can I stay with you?" He whispers.

"Um..." What should I say?

"I can sleep on the couch right here." He says, eyes meeting mine, begging.

"I don't wanna be alone tonight." He sounds so vulnerable that tears gather in my eyes.

"It's okay, Christian. I would never force you out." I smile reassuringly.

I take two pillows and a duvet and drag over to him. His eyes were already closing so I lift his head and place the pillow and cover him with the duvet.

His eyes had already shut and his breathing was starting to regulate. He looked so free and happy, with no worries of the world, not like the stern man I'm used to.

I smile and I'm about to walk away when he suddenly murmurs a few words that makes my smile grow even wider.

"Thank you, Ciane."

Chapter 24

I yawned and pulled the duvet away from my body, stretching slightly in the process. It took only a few seconds for my mind to recall what had occured the previous night. My eyes almost instantly falls on the couch. Christian was still slouched over, his legs dangling, them being too long for the small couch. I let out a small sigh and head to the bathroom, washing my face and exiting the room not bothering to change from my PJs. Christian had barely moved an inch, the rise and fall of his chest assuring me that he is indeed not dead after the amount of alcohol he consumed last night.

I did not even try to wake him up, even though he looks rather uncomfortable, the couch being too small for his large form. I quietly head down stairs to prepare some breakfast for the both of us. My mind drifts back to what he had said. He said they killed some people right in front of him? And his sister was taken? Taken as in killed or kidnapped? I did not even understand the entire thing. Who was killed? I had my suspicions but I just didn't want to believe or assume it's true. Based on the pure agony on his face, I couldn't even deny the chances of it being true.

I walk into the pantry and pull out ingredients to make pancakes as I try not to think about him. Lately, he's been on my thoughts more frequently and I wasn't even concerned about it. I was growing attached to the man. Many months ago, I did not even think I'd ever talk to him and now, he's occupying my thoughts and room.

I am so emersed in mixing the ingredients that I fail to hear his footsteps, until he was right there in front of me.

"What are you making?" Christian's voice startles me so much I accidentally splash the flour I was scooping on my face, completely turning me white. I don't even stop the squeal that leaves my lips.

"What is wrong with you?!" I hiss as I turn to glare at him. When he sees the mess he has created all over my face, his lips begins to twitch. He looks ready to burst out in laughter.

"Don't you dare laugh." I glare, my eyes lighting up with pure rage.

He completely disregard my warning and begins to chuckle, amused by the flour now covering my hair and face. Without any hesitation, I grab the flour and completely dump the content on his head. The rage I was feeling simmering out, a smile taking it's place on my lips.

"Now you can laugh at that." I smirk, pleased when his mouth drops open, brows raising so high, eyes following suit. His expression elicits a loud laugh from my lips. His hair, face and black shirt have almost turned completely white. He deserves it.

His expression completely switches and a mischievous grin forms on his lips. No! I take a step back. He grabs the sugar I had placed on the counter and without any second thought walks over to me and pour the content on my head.

He did not!

"You. . .you. . ." I mumble, not knowing what to do. I grab the eggs and hurl them at his face in complete anger. He isn't fast enough and they crack on his face, before dripping down.

Soon enough, we are caught up in it all as I hurl every ingredient I had placed on the counter, even the pancake mix on him and he does exactly the same.

I did not even realize I wasn't angry anymore. I did not even note that I was actually smiling genuinely, and a small one occupying his lips too. I didn't even realize that all the ingredients I had placed on the counter had completely disappeared, the kitchen walls and floors being occupied by said ingredients.

I take a step towards Christian and before I could even stop it, my feet slide on the pancake mix on the floor. I grab the only thing that can stable me, Christian, and he too slides making the both of us plummet to the floor.

My eyes widen comical as I stare into his eyes. He looks towards me and I stare back. Before I can stop or hold it in, a chuckle leaves my lips, turning into full blown laughing, the whole situation utterly and purely ridiculous.

"This is such a mess," I say mid chuckle as I glance at Christian who's already staring at me, a smile spread on his lips, eyes light and happy.

"Yeah, but this is entirely your fault." He slightly grins.

"No, you sneaked up on me and almost gave me a heart attack. This is definitely your fault." I emphasize.

He only shakes his head at me, a smile there occupying his lips. He tries to get up, only for him to slide once again down. He laughs slightly and pushes himself up once more and he's successful. He holds out his hand for me to take and I don't hesitate as I place mine on his. He pulls me up and drags me away from all the mess made.

When he lets go of my hand, I turn and stare at the now completely ruined kitchen with no breakfast in sight.

"This is going to take forever to clean." I groan rubbing my forehead only to smudge it with the flour covering my hands.

"Don't worry, I'll clean everything up." Christian offers and I don't even reject the offer.

"Of course you should. You did this." I state. He goes to speak but I cut him off, "But first, I'm going to shower."

After a long shower, I head back down and see Christian already clearing the mess, a clean outfit adorning his form. We silently clean the mess both of us lost in our own thoughts. It only takes a about an hour to completely get rid of the eggs, sugar, salt and the mix off the walls, floor and just everywhere.

When we were done, I head to the living room and lay my head on the couch when Christian walks in and speaks,

"I'm sorry," the words are whispered and I stare at him in confusion.

"What for?" Because of the mess we made?

"The other night. For drinking and bothering you. I vaguely remember most of it." He mumbles, rubbing the back of his neck sheepishly, a slight pink hue occupying his cheeks.

"It's not necessary, really." I offer a smile lighting my lips.

"No, but It should not have happened."

"I'm not judging you if you're worried about that. It didn't bother me at all." I smile. I wanted to inquire about everything that happened and what he said about his sister and the other people that died but I remain quiet.

He's quiet for a while before answering, a small barely there smile flashing on his mouth.

"Okay, if you say so, still I'm sorry." This isn't the Christian from a few months back. He's clearly transformed so much.

He walks away, but before he can fully exit, he turns a smirk I have never seen on him forms on his lips.

"And I meant what I said about you."

My mouth drops open and I stare at his retreating figure a look of utter bewilderment taking home on my face.

Chapter 25

T he words that left Christian's lips lingered a while longer in my brain for reasons I couldn't understand myself. He said he meant it and I remember almost vividly what those words are.

You're really beautiful.

They weren't supposed to affect me or linger that much in my brain but I couldn't stop my thoughts from floating back to him over and over again. It had been two days since he confessed that he meant it. I should know better after what Exus did to me but at them same time, I couldn't stop thinking of him.

He has done nothing to warrant or occupy my mind, but he is there, holding my thoughts captive.

"Are you even listening to me?" Christian snaps me from my thoughts.

I had somehow managed to convince him to watch another movie with me, this time the moving being his choice. He didn't even resist or refused. He even looked quite eager for it. He settled on Spiderman: No Way Home. I hadn't watched it yet and somehow I was looking forward to it. Now, thirty minutes later, I have no idea what it entails.

"What did you say?"

"Don't you want some popcorn?" He hands me the bowl and I smile taking it from him.

"What are you thinking about?" Christian asks.

My mind goes back to when he was drunk a few days ago. Will he get mad if I ask about it? Basing off the reaction he had the last time I asked, I was feeling quite cautious. I didn't want to set him off again. Even so, I couldn't help but ask anyway.

"Can I ask you something?" From my tone I knew he knew what I was planning on asking is quite serious, so he only gives me a solemn nod.

"What happened to your sister?" It comes out as a whisper, almost impossible to hear.

"You know you don't have to answer if you don't want to. I'm just curious because you mentioned her the other day." I continue before he could respond.

He is quiet for a few seconds.

"I don't know if I'll ever be able to talk about it, really." He mumbles and I instantly feel bad about it.

"Ignore me, I'm sorry." I apologize, giving him a small smile which he returns, although obviously fake.

"It's okay, Ciane. I get where you're coming from. I'd be curious too." He says, his lips widening the smile.

This wasn't the Christian from a while back who was always mad, angry and always completely detached. He is talking to me, even reassuring me. I like this new version of him.

"What I can tell you though is that it wasn't good and there was nothing I could do to stop it from happening." He mumbles, eyes falling on the tv that was still playing the movie.

"Is she. . .gone?" I hesitantly ask, afraid of the answer.

"Dead? No I would have felt it but she was taken, kidnapped before I could save her." He says, his voices filled with pain.

I remain quiet and he does too. Our eyes flip back to the tv still playing the movie. What's going on?

"Is it okay if we restart it, I have no idea what's going on?" I chuckle slightly breaking the silence.

"I knew you weren't watching it!" Christian chuckles as he restarts the movie.

"I know you weren't too so don't blame this on me," I grin.

He returns it and I get completely emersed in the movie.

I slowly gather the plates in a pile, taking as much as I could to the dining area. My duties weren't heavy this past two weeks because the alpha has not been here. Beta Jonah was left on duty and he is the only good person in this pack. The only one who has ever stood up for me. So, the punishments had lessened too.

Alpha and his sister disappeared with no word to either Jonah or his gamma, Charles. I had inquired from Jonah who revealed he knew nothing of his whereabouts. I couldn't be more happy. It meant less beating, not completely gone but less because Alpha is the main abuser.

I hum a light tune as I take a step towards the dining room. I slowly place the large pile on the table, a small smile slipping to my lips. However, one plate from the pile slides down the table, shattering immediately when it hits the floor. Any other day, I'd be terrified of the consequences but he isn't here. I could almost sigh in relief.

Before I could walk back towards the kitchen, I'm grabbed by my neck from behind. I didn't sense him! How couldn't I? Have my senses weakened that much?

The scent flows to my nose and I completely freeze. He's back! He's back with no warning, with no letter of his arrival.

"Al. . .alpha?" I stutter, trying to pull away from his grasp, only it tightens piercing painfully into my skin.

"Omega," he grunts, his voice colder than usual. The emptiness in those words sends my heart palpitating so hard, I almost pass out.

"Wh. . .what can I do for you, alpha?" I say, my words shaky and full of fear.

"Did you just break the plates?" His voice calm.

"It slipped, Alpha. It's just one plate. I'll pick it up." I whisper the terror engulfing my whole being.

"Just one plate?" With one quick motion, he turns me around and I almost pass out at the utter darkness that is his eyes. Completely dark, soulless and empty. It scares me so bad that I instantly fall to my knees, begging. It was only one plate, right? He can easily replace it, can't he?

"I'm sorry, alpha. Please forgive me. I am so sorry." I plead, my eyes already gathering heavy tears. This past two weeks have been the best with him now here to be seen. I was almost, almost having fun.

"Do you know how much money I spent on this plates, on this pack, on anything that entails my pack members? Are you planning on destroying everything on this pack and say it doesn't matter? Tell me runt, do you feel happy destroying the things that I purchase, that are definitely not yours?" He snarls, his teeth growing out of his gums.

It didn't make sense to me. It makes absolutely no sense but the amount of terror that washes over me that very second leaves me sobbing, clutching my knees tightly. I could feel my stomach drop, a feeling of pure, untampered agony feeling my heart, soul and body. I wasn't escaping his wrath, was I?

"I am sorry, alpha. I didn't mean what I said, I did not mean it!" I beg, tears falling down my eyes in pure pain. He had not inflicted any on me and yet, at that moment, everything hurt.

"It seems like my little omega hasn't been obedient this past weeks. You're nothing, slut. You're gum stuck under my shoe, I can easily dispose of you!" He smirks, the expression so cruel on his face, I almost hyperventilate. He looked dead.

Without any warning or hesitation, I feel his combat boot make contact with my stomach dragging the little oxygen left in my lungs. He does it again and again until I could barely feel my body. He grips me by my hair and I could feel him pluck some from my scalp. He pulls me up until my face is inches away from him.

"You're nothing, nothing you hear?" He yells, his green eyes burning to mine with pure rage swimming in his eyes. He delivers a quick punch to my face. He doesn't stop. He lifts my frail body and hits my face hard on his knee sending me rolling on the floor. My vision begin to fade yet he keeps going as he spews words of hate and disgust at me.

"Alpha what are you doing?" A voice yells and I could barely hear or feel. My vision had began to fade, everything disappearing slowly from my grasp.

"You're going to kill her!" The voice yells, horror and shock evident in his voice.

"Stay away from this, beta!" Alpha's voice screams back.

I close my eyes praying for it all to end, for the goddess to take me like she did my parents. For all the agony, pain and sorrow to end. I pray for my life to end right then and there.

It's not answered.

Instead, I feel a hard and sharp kick to my head that instantly turns my world dark.

I cannot stop the loud gasp or the instant flow of tears down my cheeks. I thought they had stopped. I thought the feeling of pure misery had stopped, the feeling of helplessness, that feeling of pure despair. I thought they had all stopped but I was so wrong. Oh, so wrong. I hate him, I hate him so much.

I could almost still feel his hands on me, the metallic taste of my blood flooding my mouth, the throbbing of my bruised face. I could almost feel it all.

My throat begins to close up, the need to breath getting harder and tougher, almost impossible. I couldn't make anything out from my already fading vision as I begin to gasp for air and try to control the sobs leaving my lips.

I had promised myself not to cry, not to think about them but no matter how much I try, he can never really leave me. He is embedded to my mind, tattooed to my soul. He scarred me so bad. How am I supposed to move on from it all? Am I lying to myself? Will I ever escape from him? From all the pain and torture he inflicted on me. He enjoyed my pain, he enjoyed my suffering, he savored my pain and grinned at my misery. How could I ever forget that, forgive that?

"Ciane?" His voice is only but a whisper.

I had not moved from my spot on the couch in the living room. I did not even realize I had dozed off on the couch and that Christian wasn't sitting next to me anymore. I could feel his light footsteps padding on the floor as he neared me. I had not cried in a while. I had refused to, but now I am breaking and he is here to witness how messed up I really am.

I couldn't breath. I draw breath from my lips but it's not enough. It doesn't get to my already begging lungs. In my right mind, I would have realized I was having a panic attack.

"Ciane, goddess!" Christian rushes to my side and immediately engulfs me in a hug, his masculine scent wrapping itself around me like a safe cocoon.

"It's okay, you're safe. I'm here." He whispers, his voice so soft and gentle, I almost break down once more.

"It's okay, Ciane. I am here. You're safe, you're okay." He assures, as he soothingly brushes my hair with his fingers.

"Listen to my heartbeats, sweetheart." He whispers, his voice like music to my ears.

I press myself firmly to his chest and concentrate on the thrumming of his heart, the rhythmic synch. The stable thumping, the strong beating of the organ.

I had never had anyone to hold me after all the nightmares I've had over the years and at that moment I'm so grateful for him. For the little support he's offering me. The support I have barely received all my life. My lungs suddenly begins to function, air finally rushing to deprived lungs, granting me relief, only for pure exhaustion to hold me captive in it's clutches.

"I thought they had stopped. I thought they'd gone away but I was wrong. I was so wrong." I stutter, my eyes gleaming with tears, the raw emotions on display.

He doesn't ask or comment but he holds me a little bit tighter assuring me he's actually there. That he's holding me at that moment. And my heart warms. My heart feels a little less empty.

<h1 style="text-align:center">Chapter 26</h1>

I stretch my hands above my head and pull the covers of my body. I could feel how swollen my eyes are after crying my heart out. The exhaustion I felt had not completely faded.

I remember almost too vividly the events that led to my current position. The nightmare and Exus being the root of my suffering. The mate that has caused enough physical and emotional scars to last me a lifetime. He has broken my heart so much that I'm not sure it'll heal. The scars littered on my body all caused by him.

My thoughts drift to Christian and how he had been there to comfort me. For the first time, someone was there for me, for the first time I had someone to assure me that it would be okay. Even though no words were exchanged, he had been there. I don't even remember falling asleep. He must have brought me to bed. My heart warms at the thought. He was growing on me. Christian is much much much more than Exus was, is and ever will.

I short yawn escapes and I leave my bed to take a much required shower. After I'm dressed, I exit the room, the smell of freshly brewed coffee engulfing my nostrils. Delicious. I hop down the stairs and I'm met with a sight I don't see every day. Christian preparing breakfast. My mind drifts to the last time I was standing there and a mischievous idea comes to mind.

Christian who had not even noticed me looked completely engrossed on the eggs sizzling on the pan. I smirk and take cautious steps towards him and do the exact same thing he did to me. Instead of screaming as I expect, his hands shoot out and grasps mine in a tight hold, his movements too quick for my eyes. I gape in awe. He's really good at this. When he realizes it's me, he lets go of my hand shooting me a small apologetic smile.

"Wow, I expected you to scream." I chuckle.

"Sorry, you caught me off guard." He says sheepishly.

"No wonder you're a good trainer. Your senses are great. I'm sorry we couldn't train today." I apologize.

"It's okay," he says, although his eyes looks a bit sad, "How are you feeling?"

How was I feeling? After last night, I didn't even know.

"I'm okay now." I give him a small smile and Christian stares at me obviously not believing me but he doesn't question it.

"Do you want some coffee?" He asks as he grabs a mug from the cupboard.

"Is that even a question? Of course I want coffee!"

He gives a small chuckle and pours the coffee to the brim into the mug. I take a huge sip, the hot liquid slightly stinging my tongue. I sigh, savoring and loving the feeling.

"Wow, you're really in love with this." He acknowledges.

"You can say that again." I grin, "Thanks." I raise the mug slightly.

He smiles and grabs two plates and places the eggs on it, a few strips of bacon and toast. He grabs both plates to the dining room close to the kitchen.

"Come," he urges and I follow him.

He places the plates on the table and pulls a sit for me. I smile and thank him. My stomach almost instantly notifies me of how hungry I am.

"Wow, this is really good." I smile as I shove the eggs into my mouth.

"Thank you."

Without meaning to, my eyes fall on him and all the things that occured floods my mind. The tears, the panic attack and him being there for me, calming me down. The thoughts of Exus. That disgusting so called mate. The man who hurt me so much and had loved doing it.

"I'm sorry."

Christian who was stuffing food into his mouth suddenly stops to stare at me.

"What?"

"I'm sorry about last night. I'm sorry that I was such an emotional wreck. You did not have to see that." I confess, my eyes meeting his for only a second.

"Why are you apologizing, Ciane? You shouldn't. I'm not mad or angry at you. I was worried, a little frightened but angry, never, not even slightly. Why would I even be mad at you?" He assures.

"But you didn't have to deal with that. You didn't have to see me in that situation." I insist.

Christian walks towards me and takes the chair next to me.

"And you didn't have to deal with me last time too. Remember I came here bruised and all and you didn't have to deal with that but you did. You helped me out. You did not even hesitate about it."

"So, you feel obligated to do that for me too?" I ask, almost hurt by the thought.

"No. I'm just saying that I would never feel bad about that. You shouldn't too." He mumbles, running his hand on his hair, his cheeks lighting up slightly, "I don't know what to say, really but you shouldn't apologize for something you didn't even have control over." He says, his tone nothing but sincere.

"Yeah, thanks." I stay quiet for a few seconds, "I thought those nightmares had stopped. I didn't think I would get them anymore. It has been a while since I got any. Since we started training, they had been almost non-existent until last night. I guess I had been too occupied, too focused on it that they stopped. I don't know why they are back now." I confess, my voice too soft for my liking. I hate feeling vulnerable and weak.

"Do you wish to talk about it?" The question is asked softly.

Did I want to talk about Exus? The same Exus that Christian seems to have some connection to? Did I want to tell him how much of a monster he really was. How much he hurt me? How much he scarred me? The man who was supposed to be my mate but most importantly, was supposed to be a fair and honest alpha but had done none of that. Who was even ever concerned about me? No one. I have had no friends, no family to call my own. Am I ready to tell Christian about Exus. Just because Christian asked if I want to talk doesn't mean I should confess all my secrets to him. I didn't know but at the same time my lips move forming words.

"Since I can remember, Exus has always despised me for reasons I still don't understand. He always found a way to hurt me, to show me how disgusting I am to him. So when my parents died, his beating got worse. He began kicking me, punching and doing any other thing to sow me how much he disliked me. If the alpha could actually beat you, of course every one else can do it to you too. So it began, people found pleasure in hitting me. I couldn't even stop it even if I tried. Only the beta, Jonah was ever nice to me but there was almost nothing he could do to stop it all." I sniffle, wiping the tears that had unconsciously falling down my eyes.

"I became an unofficial omega and soon I was moved with the omegas, who of course knew how much the alpha loathed me, slacked off and I was the one to do most of the chores. I was always the one on the receiving end of his wrath if something went wrong. They were never apologetic. They never cared honestly. It only grew worse as I grew older. And he loved it. I had never really wanted a mate, really but the final straw was when I found him. And the things that happened before that."

I recall it all, his hands on me, his lips pressing on mine with me no care in the world. I remember his hands, disgustingly running up and down my body, as he pressed himself close to me. How disgusting I felt at that particular moment. The fear I felt. The fear of being taken advantage of. The fear of losing the one thing that I alone I'm supposed to give. That was my breaking point. I had not minded the abuse, the torture, I had endured all but to be raped, I would never stand for it. I would never allow it.

"Hey hey you don't have to tell me the whole story." Christian's voice snaps me from my thoughts.

Was I ready to talk about how he almost raped me. Back then, it had not really hit me how horrible that was. How vulnerable I was back then. Now, I didn't want to even think about that man. I didn't want to be even close to him. It had been long since I saw him but the scars he left on me run too deep. Too deep.

I didn't want to talk about him anymore.

"It's okay if you don't want to." Christian assures as he takes my hand in his, grasping it tightly.

I tilt my head and stare at him, giving him a small smile. We were so close together. I could almost feel his warm breath fanning my face. I could see every detail of his perfect face right next to mine. His skin looked very smooth, too smooth with almost no blemish on it. His dark eyes if you looked closely have grey specks in them and they draw me in. Two freckles laid right on top of his noes. I had never seen those before. His eyes that were warm turns dark with an emotion I cannot fully comprehend. They run through my face, drinking in every little feature there. I see his eyes focus on the scar on the left side of my face and I feel it heat up. I did not particularly hate it anymore but I feel the urge to cover it with my hand and that's exactly what I do.

"Don't." He grumbles pulling my hand away from my face. He runs his fingers on the scar, skimming lightly through the rough bumps. I don't even try to stop my cheeks from hitting up. This felt too intimate if you ask me. Yet, I couldn't and maybe didn't want to move back.

He stops suddenly and my eyes fall on him once more. His already black eyes look even more dark, darker than I had ever seen before. Why is his face growing impossibly close? Why am I not moving away? It feel hypnotized by him. Him and only him. I couldn't push him away. I didn't want to. I was also moving closer to him. His face only a few centimeters away from mine. His lips are so close, too close and about to meet mine.

It never happens though with the loud blaring of the door's doorbell. I jump away from him, so fast I tumble down onto the floor. My eyes meet his that are wide and looks quite annoyed. I don't miss the quick flash of a smile though. Really?

Oh goddess. I cannot believe what we were about to do. What I was about to do! And I don't even regret it!

We were about to kiss.

"I'll go check who it is." I hurry away from him.

I'm completely in a daze.

I was about to-- We were about to-- Oh goddess.

I walk towards the door and without even checking to see who it is, I slam it open completely lost in thought. I look up and stare at the person.

My eyes widen so much they nearly drop out of the their sockets. What is he doing here? He stares back at me, his eyes moving all over my face as if seeing a ghost. How is he here? How did he get here?

"Ciane?"

"Jonah?"

Chapter 27

- -

"Jonah? How? What are you doing here? How did you find me! Did Exus send you? Exus must have sent you! How did you even get here? Does he know I'm here? Did you tell---why are you just staring at me?" I glare at the silent man.

His only reply is to gape at me, his eyes wide open.

"Ciane, it's really you!" He throws his arms around me, in a tight hug, cutting off air from my lungs.

"Okay okay." I pat his back in an awkward gesture.

"You're alive. I thought you died. Exus sent out pack warriors to look for you. They came up empty. I thought you were gone. I'm so glad to see you." He mumbles at my back and I sigh, my heart warming at the gesture.

"Yeah I am okay, Jon. Don't worry." I hug him back, the awkwardness disappearing almost instantly.

Someone clears their throat behind me and I turn to stare at the man who was already glaring at Jonathan. His eyes looked deadly cold and furious. I almost actually get scared.

"Who are you?" The once nice voice sounds completely cold and detached.

Jonah's eyes widen, his brows shooting almost too his hair. He takes in Christian's features and almost takes a step back. I would too. Christian looked lethal, ready to kill.

"I'm Jonah Storm, beta of Wolf Creek Pack."

An instant snarl escapes Christian's lips, his eyes glowing a bright red with pure fury. He looks mad, enraged and unstable. He moves too quickly for my eyes and he's instantly in front of Jonathan

"You!" He growls, grabbing him by his neck, pinning him to the wall. I didn't understand. Does he know Jonah?

"Why is everyone trying to strangle me?" Jonah groans as he tries but fails to pull himself away from the enraged man. His aura completely an alpha's. The pure power flooding the room feels completely suffocating.

He's an alpha?

"What the f- are you doing here?" He snarls, his words sounding too deep.

"I'm sorry but I have no idea who you are, sir." Jonah murmurs, his voice diminishing in the process.

"Is your alpha here too?! Did you lead him here?" Christian's voice is deadly.

"I'm sorry but I honestly have no idea who you are." Jonah insists, his eyes growing foggy, showing he's about to pass out. I don't dare interrupt though because I have never seen him that enraged.

"And what exactly are you doing here, beta?" The sarcasm in his voice thoroughly noted.

"I came because of this." He says, struggling to open his palm. My eyes drop to it and I catch a glimpse of a gold ring, with a red glowing ruby at it's center. What is that?

Christian goes completely still as he stares at the glowing ring. His eyes grow empty and the glare he shoots Jonathan could freeze lava.

"Where did you get that?" It's only whispered but I could tell Jonah was already losing consciousness.

"Christian, please just put him down and listen to what he has to say. I don't think him dying would actually help you or him." I advice and he growls before dropping Jonah who instantly pulls oxygen through his lips.

"You have one second."

One.

It's over.

Jonah tries to speak only nothing leaves his lips after his strangulation. Christian snarls and walks towards him to teach him a lesson. Or rather to choke him again.

"Christian, you just strangled him. Give him time to breath. I would like to know why he's here too." I glare at him.

He only huffs and continues glaring at Jonah who looks ready to pass out any moment, the rage in his eyes barely concealed.

"Why are you here Jonah?" I ask.

"I'm here because she sent me."

"Who sent you?" I ask, perplexed.

"Olivia."

"Who?" I'm even more confused.

Both are quiet and I'm about to ask again when Christian replies.

"Olivia, my sister."

My mouth drops.

"Your sister? But you said she was kidnapped?"

"Yes, kidnapped by Exus and Anabelle." His eyes ablaze with rage.

"But why?"

Why would Exus kidnap Olivia? Why would they do that? What would they benefit from kidnapping her?

"Why did she send you here?" He completely ignores me.

Christian does not sound angry anymore. Just completely empty and almost numb.

"She sent me for you." Jonah ignores him, his eyes darting to the walls.

Christian fury returns with a vengeance and before I can stop or react, he throws a precise punch to Jonah's cheek.

"And you left her there? You left her and came here on your own!?" He rages.

"No, I couldn't bring her! It was impossible! I barely made it here myself." Jonah yells back, frustration finally chipping into his voice.

"Still, you haven't told me why you have the ring on you! Why did my sister send you?" Christian growls, fixing a freezing glare on Jonah.

"She sent me to you, sir. Christian, her brother. She told me the ring will lead me to you." Jonah explains, "She wants you to come for her. Exus has her locked up in the darkest and furthest prisons in the pack. To get there you need to be part of the pack because it is almost at the heart of the pack." Jonah sounds almost mad himself.

"No no no no." Christian runs his hand through his hair, a defeated look flashing through his eyes.

It can't be that bad, right? Exus' image flashes through my eyes and I cringe. Yes, it can be that bad.

"I should have done all I could. I should have stopped it from happening." He mutters as he paces through the room. Mumbled and incomprehensible words tumble through his lips as he wears the floor with his pacing.

"How is she? How is she doing? Is she hurt? Of course she is. Exus wouldn't be that kind." He lets out a humorless chuckle, eyes concentrated on Jonah who shakes his head in anger.

I focus my eyes on Jonah whose eyes are drilling the floor, his hands clench tightly. He looks almost in pain too.

"I am not allowed into the lower cells. I went there for the first time and it wasn't a good sight. She was . . hurt and too thin. Her cheeks looked so sunken and her hair matted and her body had. . .bruises, healed and fresh." Jonah whimpers.

I immediately realize she must mean something more to him than he is letting on. He did not just come here from wherever Wolf Creek Pack is just to meet Christian. Just to look for a random shewolf's brother. The only other reason he'd show up is if. . .

"She's your mate."

Jonah's eyes widen so much as they meet mine it almost looks funny. Christian's pacing suddenly stops and before I stop him, he's already standing next to Jonah grabbing him by his neck. Again.

"Can you please stop trying to strangle me." Jonah chokes out.

"You're my sister's mate and you let her stay there!? Do you even care for her!? Are you even worried about her!? You should have stayed with her! You shouldn't have left her with Exus!" Christian screams, the surge of power returning ten times stronger. Jonah has no choice but to submit to the power he holds as an alpha. I could feel the itching need to do it myself but I resist as much I can.

He's an alpha.

"You're an alpha." Jonah voices it out, eyes still trained on the floor.

Christian immediately lets go of Jonah's neck, the aura completely disappearing leaving the barely there scent I'm used on him.

"You're an an alpha?" I question, staring at Christian expectantly for the grand revelation.

"Yes."

"And how do you know Jonah?" The question I've been dying to know.

"I don't,"

My eyes widen.

"So you attacked him for absolutely no reason?"

"I know Exus and the pack. He's beta of Wolf Creek. He's the enemy." Christian explains.

I'm from that pack too as much as I hate it. So I'm also the enemy?

"I don't follow." Jonah, who finally regains his breath, ask as he gets up from the floor.

Kidnapped by Exus and Anabelle.

"Why did Exus and Anabelle kidnap Olivia?"

"Because Exus attacked my pack, Night Star."

I'm too stunned to speak.

Chapter 28

"**W**hy?"

Why would Exus attack Christian's pack? Why would he do that? I know he's a psychopath but attacking packs?

"That's impossible! I keep track and records of the alpha's whereabouts and all the plans he has except. . ." Jonah trails off.

"Except what?" I inquire.

"A few years back Exus and Anabelle disappeared for about two weeks. He did no bother telling me where he was heading. He told no one. You even asked me about it, remember?" Jonah reveals, his eyes wide open, mouth on the floor.

I vividly remember that. When he returned, he showed me how much of a monster he really is.

Christian who has been listening in, suddenly let's out a boisterous growl before storming away, the anger radiating off of him deadly and completely scary. I'm left with a scared and out of place Jonah. I'm wise enough to let him go. Knowing that Exus has hurt his sister must be painful and there's nothing he can do about it.

"I'm sorry to be the bearer of bad news. That wasn't my intentions really." Jonah confesses, thoroughly rubbing the back of his neck, the awkward reaction duly noted.

I couldn't blame him though. IHowever I can't help but wonder what the glowing ring symbolizes. I have never seen one so intricately designed or so peculiar.

"Why did Olivia give you the ring and what does it mean?" I ask, not able to keep my curiosity away.

"She did not elaborate it to me. She only told me it would lead me to her brother. The only reason I went there was because Exus has been too lazy and too occupied to check on anything in the pack. He has always been secretive and with his current depression I found it a good opportunity to snoop around. I'm his beta for goddess's sake and I barely get any information out of him." Jonah rants, rolling his eyes in annoyance, getting quite comfortable in presence.

I cringe at the mention of Exus, the thoughts of that disgusting man floating to my mind.

"I'm sorry." It's all I can offer.

Jonah's eyes meet mine and a frown falls on his face as he studies my face rather uncomfortably.

"Exus has not been the same since that night you left. He has grown harsher and completely detached from reality. He force shifted, nearly killed a few pack members. He's an emotional wreck." Jonah says, running his hand over his dark blonde hair, signs of distress showing on his face.

What shocks me is the force shift. It's the most painful thing that can happen to a wolf. However, I fail to see how all this concern me.

"And how does that have to do with me?" I ask perplexed.

"Ciane, he's your mate. The one created for you by the goddess, surely you must even feel a sliver of concern and care for him." Jonah asks almost shocked by my nonchalance.

Concern? Care?

A dark cackle almost escape my lips with those claims.

"Jonah, you must have me confused with the Ciane that was once in Wolf Creek. I am not her. I will never be her. I don't care what happens to Exus. He means nothing to me, nothing you hear." I glare so fiercely at him he looks away instantly.

"But you can't honestly give up on him! On the pack!" Jonah pleads, as he advocates for his unworthy alpha.

A chuckle actually leaves my lips this time around. Does he not understand the meaning of hate? Loathe? Abhor? Detest?

"Jonah, why would I give a flying duck what happens to him? Why would he even cross my thoughts? You were there when he beat me! You were there when he took out his rage on me! When he found pleasure in my tears, when he laughed and tore my skin. When he left scars on my body! I have the scars, Jonah. I have them littered across my chest, across my legs, on my thighs, on my shoulder! I have them to show how much he hated me! You see this scar, this scar on my face is a reminder! Every morning I wake up and stare at the mirror, it's him I see. It's him I feel tearing through my flesh!"

"Ciane I. . ."

"No, Jonah you don't get to defend him! You don't get to pretend as if all that didn't happen. Do you know what finally broke me? Him trying to take advantage of me, his hands grabbing my wrists as he pressed his lips on mine, as he tried to push me on the bed." I had held on so much to the pain I felt.

A tear leaks down Jonah's eyes as they widen with horror.

"If your daughter was abused like I was, would you encourage her to go back to the same man that caused most of her grief? Would you encourage her to go back to the person who nearly shattered her?"

He's quiet and that's my answer.

"Do not interfere with things you'll never comprehend, Jonah. Do not try and understand the pain I felt because it is only me who will ever understand the depth of my scars." I glare at him and he has the guts to look embarrassed.

"I'm sorry, Ciane. I did not think through my words. I had never really dwelt on your pain or how much Exus hurt you. As you said, I'll never really comprehend the amount of pain you went through. I'm sorry. I did not mean to undermine or ignore what you went through. I'm really sorry." Jonah pleads, his eyes begging for forgiveness.

I wasn't exactly mad at him but he assumed that just because Exus is my so called mate, I'm obligated to be with him even if he abused me. I would rather fall into a volcano than to get with a man who never cared. Never bothered to worry about me. Not as a mate but also as an alpha.

"I will never get back with Exus. Not only because he abused me, also because he's a terrible person. As long as I can remember he found pleasure in hurting me and as an alpha it was his duty to protect me and he became my main tormentor. The cause of my wounds." I explain to Jonah who finally seems to get it. He give me a short nod but remains quiet.

Exus maybe my "mate" but he means nothing to me. I would never return to someone who finds pleasure in hurting others. In my pain. Never.

"I'm going to look for Christian." I mumble walking away from him, trying to escape the awkwardness.

Jonah had been the only person to save me, to nurse my wounds sometimes but I can't help but feel disappointed. He saw me through my worst and he wants me to go back to that man? Regardless of the changes he has made in his life, if he has even made any, it doesn't matter. What if I had not turned out as his mate? Would he have stopped the torture? Exus' face comes to mind and I know my answer. He wouldn't have. He's a sadistic bastard who deserves nothing but pain.

My anger slightly simmers down when I get closer to Christian's room. I didn't know how to approach him or how to start a conversation. By the almost non-existent scent coming from his room, I can almost tell he's in there.

"Christian?" I call out sheepishly.

There's no reply so I stand there for a few seconds before pushing the door open. I had only been here a handful of time though. I glance in and find him sitting on his bed, a shattered lamp on the floor, his bleeding knuckles already healing.

"Christian?" I prod lightly. He doesn't reply or even show any reaction.

I take slow steps towards him and parch myself on the spot next to him. I do not even know what I'm doing and without realizing I begin fumbling with my thumbs. I should probably leave instead of intruding when he obviously wants to be alone. I stand up ready to walk away from him and not look back. Only before I walk away, he takes my hand in his grasping it tightly holding me in place.

"Don't go." He whispers.

"Okay," I sit back down.

We stay in a surprisingly comfortable silence, both of us lost in our own thoughts.

"I remember when I met Anabelle." Okay not what I thought he'd say, however I squeeze his hand still grasping mine assuring him I'm actually listening. Even though it's about Anabelle.

"It was during an alpha meeting. I had gone for it with my father because he was preparing me for the take over. I had been excited for it and I did not know why then. And then I saw her, she was there, standing in a white dress, white heels and a deep red lipstick staining her lips, a grin on her lips. She looked beautiful, ethereal even, my soulmate. I was so captivated, enchanted by her. She was so perfect. When we made eye contact, it was perfect. A dream come true."

Okay, now my chest is hurting for no reason.

"It was all going so good. Exus approved of our relatives. Even my dad seem to have liked her and he hardly liked anyone." He chuckles slightly, the pain barely concealed.

"Then it all came crumbling down without any warning. One moment I'm thinking we are happy, making progress, the next my pack is no more, my parents. . .dead, sister gone." He whispers, the raw pain and unfiltered agony slipping through the words he's uttering. I grab his hand tighter than before assuring him, even though small and miniscule, that I'm there.

I instantly realize Annabelle must have had something to do with the crumbling of the pack.

A thought that I had not quite dwelt on or even realized was how did Exus attack Christian's pack if there were no warriors to back him up on it. He couldn't have destroyed the pack on his own, right?

"How did Exus attack your pack? Did he do it alone because I'm sure he did not destroy it on his own." I ask quietly.

A humorless laugh escapes Christian as he utters words that leaves me even more speechless than before.

"Hunters. He had skilled hunters with him."

Chapter 29

He had skilled hunters with him.

Skilled hunters.

The thought echoes through my mind over and over again.

Hunters.

Lust filled humans who crave blood and have an obsession with supernatural beings. The worst creatures to have ever walked the earth. To hire or work with these beings being the low of lows is disgusting and repulsive. Why would Exus ever do that? Why would he stoop so low? Why would he be so courageous to attack and massacre an entire pack?

"Why? Why did he attack your pack? What prompted such a reaction out of him?"

I knew Exus was harsh and a total lunatic but to bring down an entire pack with the help of hunters is something that I didn't think he could or would do. No one can do that without some strong motives.

"Do you want to share what happened? How it got there. If you don't feel like it, you don't have to." I explain staring at him expectantly.

Christian shuts his eyes almost painfully. He was struggling, I could tell. I could see the emotions well displayed on his face that he tries so hard to hide.

"You don't have to, Christian." I assure running my hand on his.

"No, I want to tell you. I have never talked about it and it's eating me up from the inside. I want to share it with someone, for once." He confesses, offering me a small smile.

I nod assuring him that he can stop whenever he wants to.

"I told you how I met Anabelle but not the events that followed. Everyone almost instantly liked Anabelle when we went back to my pack. My mother couldn't help but gush at how beautiful and charming she was. Even dad loved her. Everyone did except Olivia." He lets out a sigh.

"She felt as if there was something missing from her "perfect" character. She didn't believe it and I wish I had too but she was my mate. I didn't find fault and I told Olivia she was just thinking things." He scoffs, the words painful.

"A few months after we met, I asked her if I could mark her, if I could seal the bond between us because I knew she was the one I wanted to spend the rest of my life with and have kids with. I was so foolish." A cold, unrecognizable chuckle leaves his lips. "She adamantly refused saying she wasn't ready and that we should wait and I agreed. She grew so distant and cold from then on, began arguing so much with my sister it was growing alarming. At that point I think dad began suspecting that something wasn't right. She would disappear for days, coming back with bruises and heavily wounded flesh."

"I honestly did not know what was happening. I asked her what was wrong and she got mad each time. And then she requested to go back to her brother's pack and I accepted. I thought maybe a talk with her brother would help her or relax her. Our pack wasn't far from Wolf Creek and she sometimes went for a few days and I thought she was doing okay. She looked happy, elated even. And I was relieved. I wish it had been true or it had lasted."

He takes a deep breath, his eyes glazing over with tears. I could literally see the pain, rage and agony swimming in his eyes. I had lost my parents but I have never lost both my pack and my parents. It must be completely shattering.

"Then one day, she was gone. I could even barely feel her as a mate. It's like she had completely detached herself from me. At one point I thought she had died but I would have felt it.I was depressed, sad, angry and I could barely carry out my alpha duties. Mom and dad had already realized something was wrong with her. Dad was mad, mom was disappointed and angry for not realizing how much suffering I was enduring. They wanted to confront her. It never happened though." His eye go blank, numb.

He's quiet, tears gathering in his eyes the raw emotions causing a shudder to race down my spine. I have never seen pure pain in anyone's eyes, not as much as I see in Christian's eyes.

"Then came the. . . attack. It. . .it. . .all. . .happened s-so f-fast. I. . ." He was breaking.

"It's okay, it's okay. You don't have to continue." I quickly wrap my arm on his shoulder, pulling him closer to me, trying to hold the tears in my own eyes.

"I wasn't even prepared for it! No one was!" He stutters.

"I'm sorry. I'm so sorry." I mutter quietly.

He stays quiet and I do too as I occasionally rubbed his hands held tightly in mine. No one deserves to go through that.

He shuffles slightly and moves away from me, detaching his hands from mine. He grabs the lower drawer of his night stand and pulls out a ring, identical with the one Jonah had. He runs his thumb on the bright ruby stone, a slight smile slipping to his lips.

"I remember getting Olivia that ring," a laugh leaves his mouth. "She loved playing in the large forest surrounding the pack when she was young. I know it sounds quite dangerous but you couldn't stop her even if you tried. She would come back holding a variety of wild flowers, bugs and even sometimes what she called cool rocks."

A light smile forms on his lips. "She would get lost most of the time and come back tired, dirty and super hungry. Sometimes, she wouldn't even show up for hours and I would have to go looking for her. She would get a scolding and a warning not to go into the forest. She wouldn't listen. Dad tripled the security and even placed a warrior to guard her. Even then, she would evade him and cheekily laugh about it."

I can't help the smile that forms on my lips as I imagine a little girl evading an obviously trained warrior and enjoying it.

"I begged dad to make her something that would always lead her back to the pack. Something that would bring her back here. It was a ring. I gave it to her and promised her it would always, always lead her home. They were two and they attract each other. Almost like magnetic forces attracting each other. And it always worked. She found her way back each time."

"I didn't think she kept it. It was a long time ago." It's whispered.

"So that's how Jonah got here? The ring has some pull towards each other. So it was drawn to this one." I confirm and he nods, eyes meeting my own.

"Olivia knew this and the only way to save her is to bring her mate into this. Someone who can inform us where she is in that pack." Christian explains.

"So how are we going to bring her back? Knowing where she is won't help us get any closer to her or to save her." I inform him.

"That's your part, Ciane." My eyes turn to Jonah who is standing by the door, one hand shoved in his pocket, the other running through his hair, a look of guilt and shame rushing through his eyes. When did he get there and why does he look guilty?

"What do you mean "my part"" I quote.

"You'll have to go back to Wolf Creek Pack if you want to save Olivia."

Oh heck no!

Chapter 30

"**Y**ou have completely lost your mind!"

I did not yell that but I completely agreed with him.

"You cannot possibly expect her to go back to that. . .that monster of a mate." Christian rages, eyes glowing a dark yellow, almost red. He looks lethal and Jonah looks a bit petrified of his glare. I would be too.

"I love my sister and I want nothing more than to save her from that creep but sending her will only cause problems! What if. . .what if he holds her hostage too? Then what do we go after that?" Christian rages, the glare not faltering.

Jonah has the gulls to look scared and take steps back from him.

"Can we talk about this in the living room or something." He says, eyeing Christian room with disdain, and completely moving away.

"We are talking about this right now!" Christian glares at him.

I understand where Christian is coming from, I really did and going back would only make it worse or alot better. Knowing how Exus has been all my life, the chance of it going right it almost close to zero. However, I could not let another person suffer at the hands of that monster. I was a loving proof of how monstrous he can really be. I had to try.

"What is your plan, Jonah?" I ask, and Christian's eyes snap to meet mine but I don't meet them.

"Why are you even considering this, Ciane?" Christian's voice sound too low that I almost feel bad about it.

"I'm sorry Ciane but are you sure you want to listen to my plan? It can go horrible. It can become messy and Exus might even go back to being as abusive he was in the past." Jonah explains, his eyes meeting mine and the emotions there I can easily read. Deep down I can see he wants to save his mate. He wants to be with her. I can only imagine how hard this must be for him. Knowing that she's down there and there's nothing he can do.

"She doesn't have to do anything!" Christian chips in glaring at Jonah who doesn't even meet his eyes.

"It is my choice to make, Christian. I really don't want to go back but I need to. I cannot let your sister go through what I'm going through!" I turn to him, finally meeting his eyes that's pleading for me to understand him. And I try to. I do but I knew my choice.

"But it means going back to that bastard! He left that scar on your face!" Christian rages, his eyes filled with pain. I was the one who was hurt, he shouldn't understand it.

"I know, Christian! I know! I think of what he has done almost every single day of my life. Every day I wake up I think of all the wrong things he has done to me. All the hurt and pain I've gone through in his hands. What I would do if I ever met him. Would I be the same person he hurt and discarded? I don't know what to feel but I need to do this. Your sister does not deserve to go through what I went through. She doesn't deserve to suffer at the hands of such a horrible man." I explain, my eyes falling on him.

He looked tortured, angered and in pain. I did not understand why. This is my pain, this is my own suffering and I want to handle it on my own.

"I hate the thought of you going back there!" He whispers, eyes straying away from mine. This was getting too emotional, too personal.

I turn to look at Jonah only to be met by the empty spot he had been occupying. When did he leave?

"You shouldn't worry, I can handle it. I have been handling it for a long while now." I offer him a small sad smile which he doesn't bother returning and mine drops.

His eyes meet mine in with a heated look and emotions I had never seen flow through them. Emotions I cannot comprehend no matter how much I try to. I cannot decipher any of them and I remain perplexed. Christian had been so cold during those first days and now its like something switched and he's a completely different person.

"Okay," he relents, "but if you don't come back with Olivia I'm coming to that pack."

I almost chuckle at the serious look on his face. He always used that during training.

"Okay but I think he'll kill you if he sees your face." I offer.

"I'm serious, Ciane."

I don't offer him a reply.

"We should go look for Jonah. I didn't even hear him leave."

I say as I walk to the door and towards the living room where I find Jonah seated.

"I thought I'd give you some space." He gives a smile.

"It's okay." I return it. "I have decided to go with your plan, what is the plan?" I ask taking the couch a bit further from him while Christian remains standing shooting daggers occasionally at Jonah, who doesn't bother even looking at him.

"I told you how Exus has been mopping around after you left and feeling depressed. He's become so messy and full of pain that he stopped performing his duties as an alpha, he's drunk and only keeps muttering 'mate'. He doesn't even know your name, can you believe it?" I'm not shocked by it. He had spent his existence cursing and hating on me.

"Anyway I think we should utilize his weakness right now. All he wants is to have you by his side and for you to return. He's so desperate to have you with him. And if I bring you back to him, I'll definitely have his trust. He will let his guard down if you're around and Olivia and you can escape." Jonah explains using his hands to describe it all and it looks too funny.

"Okay, even if Exus is depressed or whatever, what will be your explanation when I show up? And when you show up, what will you tell him? Where did you disappear to? How long have you been gone anyway and how far is Wolf Creek?" I rant finding a few holes in Jonah's master plan.

"Okay, I'll just tell him I found a lead on your whereabouts and I had not wanted to give him false home in finding you so I decided to follow it on my own because I care for him and the pack. And Wolf Creek is about three days run in your wolf form. Your basically two states away."

That shocks me. I know I had ran for a while but I didn't think I got that far.

"And about my welfare, I don't look as bad as I was before so what about that?" I corner him.

"Easy, you got help from a human after running for a while. Chri- his scent is barely on you so he'll probably ignore it just glad your back with him."

"Wow, you had planned all this in your head, right?" I almost grin.

"Well, there's still a few holes in your amazing plan, Jonah but that'll have to do. For now." Christian grumbles sending Jonah a heated look.

"You really don't like me." Jonah complains to himself, a pout almost forming on his mouth.

"When will we carry out the plan?" I ask.

"The sooner the better. I already miss my mate." Jonah says, a fond and pained look flashing through his eyes.

A growl immediately leaves Christian lips and I stare at him, shocked.

"You're lucky you're trying to get my sister out! I'd give you another punch too cave in that face." Christian lethally replies, his fist clenched at his sides.

Jeez.

"Okay okay, he gets it, Christian." I state, rolling my eyes and walking over to Jonah who looks quite traumatized.

"How do you handle that?" Jonah whispers as Christian exits the room.

I wish I knew that too.

Chapter 31

I am scared.

I can literally feel the pounding of my pulse in my head. The raw fear churning at the pits of my stomach and bubbling up to my chest.

Am I really doing this? Am I really going back?

The thoughts of the things that man has done to me rushes through my eyes giving me a vivid and gory details of all the things that had gone wrong in the past. The scars littering my back, thighs, hands and face being a constant reminder of the beast that lurks just a few miles away from me.

A new wave of fear flows through every part of me as memory after memory flood my mind. I had not anticipated to feel this scared, to feel this lost. I have trained since I came here and I know I'm better than I was before, both physically and emotionally but the thought of that man sends a cold shiver down my spine. Am I ready to face him? Am I ready to go back? Am I ready to look him in the eye? The same eyes that had found pleasure in my pain, the ones that had grinned as I bled at his feet? The answer is simple, no.

I cannot possibly go back. I cannot go back to that torment, to that place that left too many scars in me. The place that almost shattered who I am, if it hasn't already.

I stare at the small duffle bag clutched between my hands containing a few of my items. Tears begin to gather in my eyes as I imagine how horrible it's going to be when I meet him, when I come face to face with him. The fear bubbles further at the pits of my stomach and I swallow thickly trying to keep the pain down.

"Ciane, are you okay?" The voice sounds so far away as if I'm drowning, which I feel I am. Drowning in my fears, pain and agony.

"Hey, Ciane." Hands are placed on my shoulder, and my chin is lifted. The tears finally slipping down my eyes. Why am I crying? My eyes makes out Christian figure right in front of me and the concerned look etched on his face.

"Are you okay?" He whispers. Am I okay? No I am not.

"No, I am not okay." I state, my eyes flowing with tears. I don't understand why am crying. Why are my tears falling rapidly down my eyes? It has been more than a year since I saw that horrible man and yet now I feel just as vulnerable as the time I was with him.

"I don't want to go back." I sob pathetically. This isn't me. I'm not someone who cries over every silly little thing but I cannot seem to stop it no matter how hard I try.

The fear of seeing him, seeing everyone in that pack. The pack that left me to suffer on my own, the pack that enjoyed my fears and did nothing to help me, to save me from the torment, the abuse, the torture.

"I don't want to see him, to see them all! How am I supposed to deal with all that, to deal with him! What if he wants to hurt me again, to use me? I cannot go back! I can't!" My breath stutters in my throat as I hiccup embarrassingly.

"Hey hey come here!" Christian doesn't hesitate to pull me to his chest and leads us back to the living room. He pulls me closer to him, hugging me tightly.

I have never thought of how I'd feel when I go back. How disgusting it will feel if he touches me knowing that the same hands had tried to pry my clothes off, the same hands had tortured me, the same hands had hurt me.

"I cannot face him knowing how he almost forced himself on me!" I whisper, the tears not stopping.

Christian stills, his arms going rigid around me, before he pulls me impossibly close to him, his hold fragile at the same time, right.

"You don't have to go, Ciane. You don't even need to go. We can find a way to rescue my sister. There's always another way. You do not have to force yourself to meet that bastard. It's not your responsibility to save Olivia. I will find a way." Christian tries to assure me but it only makes me feel horrible.

I have witnessed first hand how terrible Exus can be. How much pain he can inflict without even trying. I did not want anyone to ever go through that ever again, especially someone innocent. I would try my best to bring her back, help her.

It finally dawns on me how humiliating this is. Crying my eyes on Christian's chest, while he tries and comforts me. Again. I pull away my cheeks reddening with shame.

"Sorry for that." I mutter, glaring at the small blotch of tears smeared at the side of his white t-shirt.

He doesn't say a word so I lift my eyes to stare at him, only to find a serious expression marring his face.

"Did. . .did he really try to force himself on you?" My eyes fall to the floor.

The memories of that night still haunt me, his hands, the gleam in his eyes, the pleasure he must have felt trying to take advantage of me.

I offer him a small nod of affirmation and his eyes darken.

"You're not going back there." He states without any hesitation.

I disagree.

"I have to go back! If I do not, your sister will still suffer! She will keep suffering. There's no other way, Christian!" I exclaim.

"No, you cannot! We can find another way! We can contact the elders, inform them of what has happened! I am still an alpha and they will listen." Christian says, eyes burning bright.

A thought comes to mind. Whenever a pack is demolished, the werewolf elders are informed and they investigate reasons for the pack's demise.

Did they ever visit Christian's pack?

"Did the elders ever visit the pack to inquire what happened?" I ask quietly, knowing it's a sensitive topic.

"I wasn't around at the time." He visibly winces his finger twitching at his side, before his fist clench. "I heard they ruled it out as hunters." He scoffs.

You would think they would offer more help to the pack.

"Were there any survivors apart from you and your sister?"

His eyes grow cold and the scent of blood suddenly hits my nose. My eyes scan his body looking for any injury until they land on his fist. His claws were already puncturing his palm. I am ready to take back my question or to tell him to ignore it when he answers.

"When an alpha disappears or leaves the pack, the pack will be in utter chaos and if there were any other survivors, they fled, went rogue or joined other packs."

He looked pained, tortured by it all. I don't ask any more question. I don't ask where he had been because he already looks mad, angry and hunted by the past.

"Can we talk about going back later?" I mutter, standing up and dragging my duffle bag back.

"Yeah, maybe later." He sounds so far away. So cold just like the days I first met him. He walks away towards the door and I stare at his retreating figure not knowing what to do.

Loud footsteps echoes right behind me before they halt when they see the duffle bag dragged back into the mansion.

"We aren't going back today, are we?" I turn to Jonah who has an understanding look on his face.

"No, not yet." I whisper.

"Take your time, Ciane. There's no hurry." He smiles. However, I could see he's desperate to have Olivia by his side.

"You don't have to hide it, Jon. I know you miss her and it's okay." I offer him a short smile.

"I do miss her but I'm not going to take advantage of your willingness to go back to that pack. I know they hurt you so bad, myself included. You willing to go back at all is a gift on its own." Jonah says, offering me a small smile that I forcefully return.

"We will go back, Jonah. I know Exus and he's a psychopath." I offer him a sad look.

"Olivia is strong and I know we will save her." He says, a fond and loving look flashing through his eyes.

"You really like her, don't you." I shoot him a genuine grin and he has the guts to blush.

"Aw, you're blushing!" I laugh.

"Shut up!" He grumbles.

"We will get her out of that pack, I promise." I assure him and myself.

I would never let anyone go through what I went even if it means facing my worst fear, Exus.

Chapter 32

I am again standing staring at the wide expanse of trees covering the mansion, the small duffle bag clutched in my hand so tightly I can feel it almost snapping.

"Are you ready?" Jonah's voice sounds behind me and I offer him no acknowledgement.

A part of me wants to turn back and dive into my room and sleep for a very long time but the other part knows I can't do that. It's a journey that must be made, an important part that must be completed.

"Yeah, where is Christian?" I ask, turning to glance at him.

"He's not here. I think he's still mad you didn't go with his plan." Yeah the intricate plan to get us in a bigger mess.

"He'll get over it, we need to leave now." I offer as I hoist the bag to my shoulders.

"Are you sure about this, Ciane?" Jonah asks, his voice sounds unsure.

"No, but it something that must be done. Now come on before I change my mind, again." I exclaim walking deeper into the dark forest right in front of the mansion.

I had never left the mansion after I was attacked and now, here I am heading back to the man that had caused pain in my life. Someone who has made tears flow down my eyes so bitterly and so angrily.

"We should shift, we will get there faster." Jonah states and I freeze.

It has been so long, so so long since I was in my wolf form, the other part of me I had not let out in a long time. The urge to shift had receded back when Exus had used his alpha command to stop me from shifting. I cannot recall it. I can vaguely recall the grey and white fur that coat my wolf. A wolf that has never run through the cold forest or felt the cool dirt between their paws, the wind blowing through their fur or the dripping of the rain, nature's sweet scent.

"I cannot shift." Jonah freeze. "Exus commanded me never to shift."

"What?" His eyes so wide they almost pop out of his sockets.

He's quiet for a moment before he speaks up again.

"When you left the pack, the command also lifted so you can now do it but it'll be painful. Do you want to try? I didn't know he commanded you not to shift. I'm so sorry." Jonah explains, remorseful.

"It's not your fault and I would like to try." I state.

"Okay do you remember how to do it?" He asks and I give him a small nod.

I pull the black top and the dark skinny jeans I had on without warning Jonah. His eyes widen before he quickly turns away.

"Can I get a warning first, jeez."

I wasn't concentrating on him anymore as I pushed my human consciousness out, and letting the animal side of me to take reign. And it happens, the most intense pain I have ever experienced rushes through every bone in my body. I feel crack after crack as my body begin to take the form of my wolf. Whimpers leave my mouth as I try to suppress the pain roaming through every part of my body. I can feel the tears falling down my cheeks as I transition from human to wolf. I lay still as I breath to my shifted form. I can smell the sweet scent of the dirt covering the surface of the earth, the light breeze brushing through the thickness of my fur, Jonah's unique flowery scent, the flowing water from a river a few miles away.

"You did it." Jonah's voice floats through the thick fog of my mind and I yip in pleasure.

I have shifted once again and I cannot help but enjoy the new scents attacking my nose, every new details my eyes can now see. It's ethereal, beautiful and enchanting.

I hear the crack of bones and my eyes shift to Jonah whose bones were already aligning to form his gigantic wolf. Being a beta wolf an added advantage. His coat is a dark brown with patches of white and grey littered all over his form. He looks amazing and I can't help but nudge his muzzle with his.

"Come on, we should go." Jonah's voice echoes through my head and my eyes widen. We can mind link each other?

I don't ponder on it though so I grab my bag by my teeth as Jonah dashes into the woods and I follow suite.

It has been two whole days and I had not shifted back from my wolf form. I have been enjoying the freedom that comes from being in my fur, the beautiful scents, hunting of wild deers and rabbits. It has been an eye opening and sweet experience. I had missed out almost two whole years of being in my wolf form, the other part of me.

I was so busy enjoying the sweet natural scent of the nature that I barely noticed the shift in the air. We were approaching his territory. His pack. Wolf Creek. The scents flood my nostrils at the same time as the memories. The memories of all the pain I had encountered. The moment I had crossed the border. All of them flood my brain and I have to close my eyes to push the memories away.

"We are here, we should shift before pack patrols show up." Jonah explains and I head towards a group of trees.

My fur recedes and my flesh returns as I shift back to my human form. I quickly put on my clothes and emerge to fin Jonah already shifted and dressed.

"I did not know you could mind link me." I state.

"Yeah, alpha and beta and some gamma wolves are able to link all other wolves. It's important because if an attack were to happen, they'd be an easier way of communicating with other packs." Jonah explains, as he stares into the wide and enormous land of Wolf Creek. The pack that is responsible for my tears and pain.

"Oh that makes sense." I smile.

"I have mind linked the border patrol. They'll be here any moment."

With those words, I note the quick pounding of wolves heading towards our direction. I swallow hard, trying to subdue the pain and the uncomfortable feeling accumulating at the pits of my stomach.

Six wolves emerge through the thick trees, three in their wolf forms, the other in their flesh, clothed in nothing but basketball shorts.

"Beta Radcliffe, alpha has been inquiring of your whereabouts. You've been gone for almost a week." A dark skinned man, with short fluffy dark hair says as he stares at him, his eyes not noticing me at all. He must be new to the pack because I have never seen him before.

"I have a good reason for that, Ashton." Jonah replies, his eyes shooting to meet mine and almost instantly their eyes fall on me.

"Who are you? You look familiar." One of the pack warriors who had taken part in my torture asks as he stares at me, a look of confusion rushing through his eyes.

I had changed quite a bit I would say. My body that had been nothing but flesh and bones had now filled out and I look healthy and well kept. I looked nothing like the skinny, malnourished girl I was a year and a half ago. I had changed and I loved all the changed I had gone through.

Before he can respond, a figure emerges right behind the gathered warriors and my breath hitch. He was actually here.

"Beta, where have you been. You cannot disappear and emerge a week later with no explanation." His voice is exactly as I remember. Cold. Detached and full of nothing but malice.

"I can explain." Jonah beings glancing at me and that's when his eyes meet mine and they widen.

I meet his eyes, the cold green eyes that had hurt me, that had enjoyed ripping my flesh. The eyes that had stared into mine while he beat me to a pulp. The eyes that had shone with ecstasy as he teared and ripped my flesh with his whip and knife. I could feel my scar burn as if I was back there with him, ripping through my face, offering me a permanent reminder of who he is.

Every day you wake up, I'll be the first thing you see.

I vividly recall the words he had uttered and he had been right. The scar has always reminded me of him. The beast that he is.

"Mate?" He whispers as I see tears gathering in his eyes. Eyes that I dislike so much. Eyes that I loathe it's shade. The lightest shade of green I have ever seen and I hate it.

I don't respond and my mind vaguely registers him rushing towards me, a look of elation flashing through his eyes. I wasn't and isn't feeling the same. He is a few feet away from me and before I can pull away he pulls me towards him, holding me close to his chest alighting light sparks on my body and I hate it. I hate the sweet scent that is supposed to appeal to me but is only making me want to puke. The sparks that rushes through me that reminds me of how disgusting he really is.

His hands are touching me. The hands that have hurt me, the hands that have scarred me. The hands that nearly r*ped me, the hands that have smacked me and hurt me beyond belief. I hate it! I hate it all! I hate who he is. I hate that he thinks everything is okay. I hate that he is hugging me, I hate that hi scent is invading my nostrils. Goddess I hate him.

"You're here, you're really here!" He murmurs and I nearly puke at how soft and different his voice is. It's disgusting. It's repulsive. I want his arms off of me.

I shove him with all the strength I have in me and he has no other choice but to let me go. He stares into my eyes, hurt and remorse evident in them. I almost cackle at the emotions displayed. I wish I could say I cared anymore, or ever did.

"Can we talk about this at the pack house?" Jonah breaks the weird silence and I glance at him.

How would I handle this disgusting example of a mate. He's already so disgustingly clingy. Goddess.

Chapter 33

His eyes had not left me as we walk towards the pack house. The other warriors kept shooting looks towards me, eyes wide open with unbelief. Maximus, the warrior who had hurt me before kept gaping at me. I send him harsh glares that has him cowering away like the pathetic wolf he is. He should be intimidated. I wasn't the same person he hurt and abused without reason. I am past that.

I glare at the gravel that leads towards the pack house, the place that hold horrible memories for me, horrible unforgettable memories. I glare at the gigantic house, finally noting the once white coated walls looks quite chipped off and dirty. I guess the park slave not being around was showing.

"No one should know of my mate's return until I announce it." I cringe at those words directed at the warriors. The reply with a nod, a short bow as they leave.

"Let's head to my office." Exus mutters and we follow suit. Jonah slips his hand to mine, offering me a gentle squeeze. I return the gesture.

I could easily note the changes that have already occured since I was gone. The walls look dirty and unkept. I always kept everything neat.

"I'm sorry this place looks bad." Exus offers and I don't reply.

We take the stairs towards his office and I have to push so hard for the memories not to surface. The memories of all the beatings, the yelling and screaming by the man who was supposed to protect me. Exus leads us to his office, gently pushing the door to his office open and letting Jonah and I get it before be follows suit. The office looks terrible with what looks like broken chairs and shattered vases.

"I apologize about this." Exus mutters, running a hand through the back of his neck.

"Please take a sit." He shoots me a small grin which I don't acknowledge or return causing his to instantly fall. He takes a seat on his own seat and openly stares at me, completely ignoring Jonah.

"I'm so happy you have returned, mate." I cringe at the words.

"Ciane. My name is Ciane. I am not your mate and never call me that!" I grit, shooting him a freezing glare. He has the guts to look embarrassed and look away. Of course he has never learnt what my name was. He had had pleasure calling me disgusting names.

"Can I give you a tour around?" He asks, wincing almost instantly the words leaves his mouth. I knew this house like the back of my hand and I wasn't going to need a tour but in order to save Olivia, I'd have to pretend to get along with him. I'd have to pretend as if I actually care about him. The thought makes me cringe and nauseated.

Not getting a response from me, Exus eyes settles on Jonah who shoots me a small smile.

"How did you find her? I have been looking for her for over a year now and why didn't you even tell me you'd found her!" Exus' voice rises with every word he utters, until he's finally just yelling.

Of course he's still that bitter man I remember.

"Calm down, Alpha. I will explain every thing you need to know." Jonah states calmly, "Or better yet, Ciane can explain it you."

At the mention of my name, his eyes meet mine and they soften so much, it makes me want to puke. I did not want his eyes on me, I didn't even want him near me. At all.

"I went away for a good reason, Alpha Exus." I stare at him and he flinches at the name, "It was actually entirely your fault. You beat me up, hurt me and did alot of nasty things. I only came here because Jonah here forced me to be here." I lie, easily.

"Where did you find her? Why didn't you tell me anything?!" Exus glares at Jonah who looks away from his intense eyes.

"You've been so angry for so long that I didn't want to give you false hope about finding her. I found a lead on her whereabouts and decided to follow it on my own. I know if was reckless but I only wanted the best for you and the pack," Jonah states, eyes meeting mine shortly before he stares at Exus, " I found her living a few miles away in a human town. I had to literally beg her to come back. I assured her that you were no longer the cold hearted man that you were before." I almost gag at those words.

Not the man he was before? He is exactly the man he was before and if he is even a little bit wise, he should already know something's off and that's there's no way I'd ever come back here willingly.

Instead of thinking thoroughly about the rather vague and very unbelievable story, his lips part in a huge grin before he shoots up from his seat and embraces Jonah whose eyes widen so comically.

"Thankyou! Thankyou so much for bringing my mate home!" His voice is full of emotion as I stare at the two. Jonah awkwardly pats his back, eyes darting to meet mine, almost in panic and I smirk. He should suffer for telling the creep I came here because of him.

When they finally part, I glare at the said man.

"Don't think you are forgiven, Alpha Exus. Everything you did to me, everything this pack did to me can never be forgotten." His face falls, "I'll give you one month to prove to me, you have changed and that this pack will not harm me ever again." A grin forms on his lips, and he tries to hug me too. I quickly side step, barely escaping his arms.

"And no hugging. I hate hugs." I didn't. I just hate his.

A small sad smile forms on his lips, and he speaks up, " I am very very sorry for all the things that I did to you. You did not deserve it at all and I will spend the rest of my life, trying to prove myself to you, Ciane. And please just call me Exus, you're my mate."

My fist clench at my side as I stare at the disgusting looking man. I have to hold in dark words I want to utter to his pathetic face. I have loads of things I want to spew and curse at him but I offer him a nod, that means nothing. He means nothing. Whatever bond we had died before it even began. It died the day he touched me, the day he hit me.

Before he can make any more comments, the door to his office slams open and the scent almost instantly assaults me. I grit my teeth so hard, trying to suppress the cold rage bubbling to the surface.

"Well, the lost mate, finally returns! Jonah, where did you get this one?" She inquires, her voice still as cold as I remember, still as void of life.

"Great to see you too, Anabelle." Jonah murmurs.

"And what was your name again, omega?" She sneers as she takes the small couch next to Exus'desk.

She looks just as I remember, although her eyes look dark, empty and lifeless. The color green of her eyes reminding me why I really hate that shade. Her brown hair looks slightly matted but overall, she's still the same bitch I remember.

"Anabelle, shut up! Don't you dare disrespect my mate, ever again! She has a name, best you learn to use it." Well that's a first for him.

"She's been here for what? A few hours and you're already siding with her?" Anabelle's eyes meet with my own and I glare back. I was no longer the weak female she remembers me to be. I refuse to be, I refuse to be weak ever again.

"She's my mate! You are beneath her!" Cringe.

"Why did she even come back? Do you honestly think she came back for you?" Anabelle taunts as she glares and smirk at Exus who looks ready to explode.

"Yes, she did! We are mates and there's nothing stronger than that. If you have nothing to talk about, leave!" He yells and for only a small moment, I see hurt in Anabelle's eyes.

"I know she did not. And I will find our what she's here for! Mark my words." Anabelle says, as she exists the office, shooting me a freezing glare that I happily return. She has the guts to look shocked.

"I'm sorry about her." Exus says giving me a small smile. This is getting weird.

"It's okay, can I get the tour around the pack that you had offered before?" I offer a small forced smile, and a gigantic one appears on his mouth making me instantly regret it.

"I would love to. Jonah can accompany us." He forces the words out. I'm pretty sure he just wants me alone with him and for our plan to work, it'll have to be him alone.

I give Jonah a subtle shake of my head and he immediately understands.

"It's okay, alpha. I need to get back home. My parents must be going crazy right now. It is okay with you, Ciane?" Jonah asks and I give him a nod.

Jonah's parents had already returned? The last I heard of them was they were travelling the world, right after Exus' father died.

"Yes, I can tour with Alpha Exus." He gives a short nod and exits leaving me with the disgusting man.

"So where to?"

Chapter 34

"**W**herever you want to go." He gives me a smile and let's me exit the office first. I walk towards the grand pack lands coated in gigantic trees that acts as a hiding spot for the wolves to transform. It looks very familiar but at the same time, not. It has been almost an year and I can still remember racing through them, trying to escape him. The man currently shooting me a huge grin. I stare at him and immediately cringe.

"A tour of the pack lands would be nice." I mutter, my eyes moving over all the nicely painted houses that mated members of the pack live. They look gorgeous. Back then when I was still silly I would have wanted to live in one with a mate. Now, I just want to live this place as soon as possible.

"This land stretches for miles for wolves to run and to hide us from the world too." He says.

I know all these things but I offer him a silly nod. He knows I know all these things and he's only stalling in order to keep up the conversation. I am too, but for different reasons.

It takes about twenty minutes for us to roam around the pack talking about nothing in particular. I could easily note how he avoids heading towards the cells just not far away from the pack house.

"Wait, we haven't gone to the cells. I have never been to that one close to the pack house. I'd like to take a look at that." I voice my thoughts.

He suddenly stops walking, his back going rigid, his shoulders tensing. He turns back, offering me a very fake smile.

"Why.. why do you want to go there?" He stutters, already proving to me that he's hiding something.

"You were giving me a tour, Alpha Exus and a tour means taking me everywhere." I retort, my eyes holding his before he looks away.

"But. . .The cells, they holds nothing of your interest, really." He responds, his hands fisting at his side.

"That's even the more reason to go there." I offer him a grin and his eyes soften slightly.

"I don't want you going there," he says and I glare.

"Why? Are you trying to control me?" I ask, acting shocked by his behavior. I honestly expect nothing from him.

"No, but there's something down there. Something I cannot show you."

Ugh, this is getting tough.

"But, you said I'm your mate, right? Why are you hiding things from me. You said you have changed. You refusing to take me there just shows me you haven't changed. You said we should trust each other. Give me a reason to trust you!" I insist as I stare at the building that looks so deteriorated. I can't believe Jonah's mate has lived there.

Exus stares at me for a few seconds, rush of emotions displaying on his face before he sighs and rubs his temple.

"Okay, I promise you whatever is down there is for a good reason." He states as if assuring himself more than me.

"What? Do you have someone down there or something?" I chuckle slightly. He doesn't reply as he leads us towards the cells. The cells holding Christian's sister. Jonah's mate.

It takes only a minute for us to get to the heavily guarded door. I had never wondered why no one was ever allowed here accept Exus and Anabelle.

"Open the door, Daniel." Exus orders one of the guard who slightly bows before carrying out the door. It creaks, the sound horrifying and screechy like in movies.

Exus pulls out his phone from the back of his pocket and turning it on, slightly illuminating the room. I take note of the flight of stairs heading underground. A sudden horrible thought comes to mind and I see myself in the same situation I was before. It has always been him flooding my nightmares, him hurting me.How can I walk with him down there knowing he can hurt me.

"Come on," he says, turning around. His face meets the horrified look on mine and he sighs, hurt flooding his face. He shouldn't feel hurt. He should feel worse.

"You don't trust me." He states, "Daniel can come with us." He says. The guard whose not far from us walks towards us.

"Of course, alpha."

It doesn't help but I go with it anyways. The steep stairs lead to a more horrifying looking cells. The scent of death and decay emits from every inch of the building. My nose scrunches with disgust. Our footsteps echo through the building, almost deafeningly.

Exus leads me to the furthest part of the cell and the closer we walk, the harder my heart begins to beat. I didn't know what to expect. Knowing Exus it wouldn't be anything good at all. I am not wrong. Tears almost in an instant gather in my eyes as I stare at the girl sleeping on the corner of the cell.She looks emaciated, thin and completely unhealthy. The clothes she has on look worn out, dirty and too big for her. She lays on a small bed, a small mattress and a flimsy blanket barely covering her. The tears almost fall down my cheeks when I see her back that's ridden with scars, both new and old. She looks terrible. I cringe at all the torn parts of her oversized shirt. She looks to be about my age but I cannot be sure. If she's about my age then that means she's been here since she was fifteen. Basically a child. Olivia.

"What did I do now, Exus? Your visits are becoming rather frequent." The girl's voice is cold, emotionless and void.

I turn to stare at the man who calls himself Alpha. He basically imprisoned a child. A girl who I'm sure has nothing to do with whatever feuds he has with Christian's pack. He does not even looked ashamed of his actions, he doesn't look remorseful holding a young woman captive.

Getting no reply, the girl lifts herself up from the floor, the action taking almost all her strength and she nearly plummets back. I wince at the slight display of pain on her face. Her eyes meet Exus, Daniel before dropping down to meet mine. I almost gasp at how identical she looks to Christian. There's no doubt she's Olivia.

Her eyes scan my form, taking in every bit of me. Her face scrunch slightly before they focus on Exus once more.

"And who is she? Don't tell me it's another one of your play toys?" She grins, the look too cruel on her face.

This sets Exus off making him release a large and definitely unnecessary growl. Very immature of him.

"Don't talk to my mate in such a tone," he yells, the sound almost deafening.

Olivia's eyes widen slightly before she burst into a full blown laugh, her cackle echoing through the room. I stare at her in utter perplexity. What is so funny about the situation? I move closer to the cell and Exus tries to grab my hand and I easily slip through.

"Oh, so you're that female that ran away. The one that escaped his abusive mate. You came back? For what? You must be very desperate to have come back to such a pathetic man." She smiles and I almost get scared. She looks too emotionless at the moment. As if she's no longer afraid of Exus or even death.

Before Exus can overreact again, I turn and shoot him a nasty glare. His only response is a huff as he looks away. I stare at her, hoping to convey emotions through my eyes, to let her know that I'll be breaking her out soon.

'I'm with Jonah' I mouth hoping she can read my lips.

I know she understands as her eyes shines with recognition. Her eyes move to Exus once more and a small smile slips to her lips.

"Remember when I told you all the bad things you've done will come back to bite you." She whispers, ominously, "Well the time has come."

I turn to look at Exus and I'm surprised to see a hint of hesitance in his eyes. He has a far away look and before I can ask what it is, it's gone.

"You're never leaving, Olivia. Not after what you did." He responds vaguely and without my permission, he takes my hand in his lighting up those disgusting sparks that remind me he's my mate, and pulls me towards the stairs.

I am too confused and too shocked to even act as I try to make sense of the situation.

Chapter 35

"What the freak was that? And who is she?" I glare at the man standing right in front of me, not even appalled by the fact that he has a vulnerable woman in his cells. A woman who looks to be in poor health and very young.

"Her name is Olivia and she's my prisoner." Really?

"Of course she's your prisoner, what the heck did she do? She looks pretty young."

"I can't tell you." He says, his voice sounding too calm.

"Why?" I continue, "Why are you so adamant about not sharing the information with me. I'm sure it must be very bad if you had to isolate her."

"I cannot tell you why! I promised her it'll only be between the two of us." He says, a grim look flushing through his face. She promised Anabelle? Of course he did.

"How long has she been down there?"

He hesitates.

"Five years."

It still manages to shock me.

Five years of isolation? Torture? Pain? Five years not knowing ones family. Not knowing if their family made it or not. How did he even take her? How did he manage it without anyone knowing all this? So while I suffered she did too. While I went through pain and hell, she was also going through it.

"Does the pack know? Does the pack know you have someone down there?"

"No, only a few guards and Jonah recently found out. You are to tell no one of this. You said you wanted me to trust you, showing her to you is me trusting you to keep this a secret."

I already knew though.

"What do you plan on doing with her? You can't keep her hidden forever? Whatever she did must have been too great then." I hint and he only looks away.

Why does he look guilty if he is sure what she did justifies her punishment. Why does he look conflicted?

"I don't know. I'll eventually have to find a permanent solution to it." He says, no remorse evident in his voice and I gape at him.

"You mean. . .kill her?" I'm too shocked.

"If it is necessary, yes!" He does not hesitate.

"Why does she deserve to die? You not actually explaining to me why she's there is very strange. Unless you have no idea why you put her there." He looks away.

"Why is she there, Exus?" I ask, for the first time using his name. He looks surprised and almost transfixed by it.

"You used my name." He smiles and I don't bother to offer one back. He makes me cringe.

"Yes, why is she in there? What did she do to deserve so much punishment! I saw her back! The scars that litter her back! I saw how thin she is. The limp she had! Tell me why you deserve a second chance! Tell me why I shouldn't just leave after seeing another person in almost the same exact position I was an year ago? What justifies your actions because after what I witnessed I'm actually second guessing my decision to give you a second chance." I state, my eyes staring into his that turn grim as I keep speaking.

"I am so sorry for what I did and I know my apologies will never cover for what I did and I will spend the rest of my life apologizing for everything I did." He doesn't answer my question.

"Olivia hurt my sister! She caused so much suffering to her and I vowed that she would pay for it!" Oh my goddess!

"What did she do, Exus! You are not answering my question! You keep avoiding answering it! What did she do?!" I glare and he lets out a sigh.

"She killed Anabelle's baby, my niece."

"Hey, Ciane are you okay?" I barely register his voice.

"Yeah, Alpha Exus just told me something shocking."

"About?" Jonah asks taking a sit besides me.

"Olivia." His shoulders go rigid, hands curling into a fist, breath becoming quite laboured.

"What about Olivia?"

"He said she killed his niece." I'm still in shock.

"What?!" He screams.

"Yeah, I know. I had the same reaction." I sigh rubbing my palms together trying to make sense of all this. It's getting complicated.

Was this baby Christian's and Anabelle's? Most probably, yes. But if so, wouldn't Olivia have loved her niece too? And how did she kill the baby? The way Christian talks passionately about her, I doubt she'd kill her own niece. Her brother's child.

"That makes no sense. Olivia evidently loves her brother. You should have seen the look on her face when she talked about him. She misses him alot." Jonah states, confirming my thoughts.

"Yeah, Christian talks about her too. He loves her. Something isn't adding up here. Something is wrong." I state, biting on my lower lip.

"Did Exus tell you anything else?" Jonah asks, eyes alittle foggy with emotions.

"No, he dropped that bomb and walked away. I think he went to go and cry or something. He looked pretty depressed." I chuckle, the image displaying in my mind. Is it wrong that I actually don't care about him at all. Him showing any type of emotion make me cringe and nauseated.

"You honestly don't care about him, do you?" Jonah asks, eyeing me curiously. I couldn't deny that.

"Not really. I don't think I've ever really cared for him. I don't think I ever will. Not that I ever want to. He honestly makes me want to puke." I speak my mind.

"What about Christian?" I almost blush.

"What about him?"

"You know I can see it in your eyes, right? You like him." He states.

"I don't know honestly. I don't know what that is."

Jonah chuckles noting the awkward and uncomfortable look on my face.

"For what it's worth, I think he's obsessed with you. He likes you alot."

"Yeah, whatever. Keep talking and someone is bound to here us." I grin, before it drops. "What are we going to do about Olivia."

Jonah is about to reply when I see her approaching us, her footsteps slow and steady. Ugh here we go again.

"What do you want, Anabelle." I ask going to stand up from the sit I was in.

"Omega." She grins

"Bitch." She scowls before turning to Jonah who looks up at her.

"Beta Jonah, what are you doing with this. . .thing." she spits, disgust clearly painted on her face.

"I did not know I was suppose to inform you of all my friends, Anabelle." Jonah mutters, eyes narrowing on the demonic female.

She rolls her eyes and they meet mine.

"I know you did not come here for my brother, omega. I will unmask you for the piece of sh∧t that you are and you will go back to being the pack's slave! I will make sure you rot in the darkest parts of this pack!" She screeches before bumping my shoulder with hers, storming away like a toddler.

How immature is she?

"Don't worry about her, Ciane. You know I would never allow you to go through that." Jonah states.

"No, I'm not worried about that. I'm worried about the fact that we don't know the truth of what happened between Christian's pack and Exus. Time is running out."

Jonah is quite for a few seconds before he speaks up.

"Olivia. Olivia must know what happened. We can ask her, however. . ."

"Yes, she must know. I'll just have to find a way down there again."

"How?"

"Don't worry, Jonah. I'll have all the information on what happened soon."

Chapter 36

"Have you settled in yet?" Alpha Exus asks, completely appearing out of nowhere. The apple on my hand slips and rolls on the floor. He stares at it and offers me an apologetic look while I offer him a blank one.

"Yes, the room is nice." I state, rubbing my neck finding the entire conversation very awkward and unnecessary.

"How was your night?" He continues torturing me.

"It was nice." I cringe.

"Have you had breakfast?" He asks again. Oh my gosh.

"You literally forced them to cook everything! It was completely unnecessary."

I wince at the memory of breakfast, the amount of food on display, the million 'good mornings' I got, and the fake smile. It left me strained and completely lose my appetite. The same members who had been responsible for my tears and pain were all pretending nothing had gone wrong. The ones that had kicked me and demanded I do every chore for them. How pathetic. I also could feel Anabelle's glare at the side of my face. Jonah and Exus were nowhere to be seen; my concern being Jonah.

"I wanted to make you feel welcomed."

"Well, you did the complete opposite! This pack spent half of my life hating and beating me! Now they are all nice and good?! No thanks! From now on I'd love to have my meals in my room!" I glare walking past him.

I could feel rage bubbling within me ready to explode. The very thought of spending any more second with them. The same people who have hurt me over and over again. The ones that have never cared for my well being. Why was I here again? Why am I going through all this? Why am I letting myself be affected by those disgusting people. I could tell there are a few new members who know nothing of what happened, however the pain and suffering I went through was real, it happened. The memory of Olivia's face flashes through my mind and a sigh escapes my mouth. I am doing this for her, for Jonah, for Christian and most importantly, me.

A sigh comes rushing out of my mouth at all this thoughts. I have lived most of my life in pain, torture but the thought of her going through the same thing over and over leaves a bitter feeling in my heart. I can't let her go through that for another more years. Olivia deserves better, she deserves more than Exus is offering.

"Hey, are you okay? What happened?" Jonah asks appearing suddenly giving me quite a fright.

"What the freak, dude! Don't do that!" I glare at the said man, speed walking towards the room I was given.

"Now I know something's up. Did something happen during breakfast? Sorry I wasn't around. Exus finally agreed to transfer a few pack members who found their mates in other packs." Jonah explains keeping up with my pace.

"Oh, okay and yes something did happen. Alpha Exus ordered the pack cooks or whoever prepares food to make almost all types of food for breakfast for me. Everyone was all nice and all and it was just so weird I completely lost my appetite." I rant glaring at nothing in particular.

"He's really trying to get on your good side, isn't he." Jonah observes and I shoot him a nasty look.

"Well he's wasting his time." I assure.

Jonah just shrugs muttering to himself. He's not quiet for long though.

"Have you decided how you're going to talk to Olivia?" Jonah questions, and I stop walking having already reached the door to my room.

"No, have you visited her yet?"

A grin forms on his lips, eyes softening, emotions flooding his eyes. He's in love.

"Yes, I did. I convinced Exus to let me handle her case. He surprisingly agreed. Now I can visit as frequently as possible." He explains.

"Well that's great! You'll just have to tell Exus that we'll be going together. I'm sure he'll agree to it." I grin up at him, the situation already fixed.

Jonah's face drops.

"I don't think he'll agree to that. Alpha Exus perceives Olivia as a threat who'll do you harm."

"I'll have to force my way in then."

"Um, how will you do that?" Jonah asks, a perplexed and shocked look flashing through his eyes.

"We'll know that when we get there so come on!" I urge, dragging him by his gigantic arm.

I'm at the last step down the stairs when his scent floods my senses. I can't really escape him, can I?

"Ciane, can I talk to you for a second?" He says eyes holding a certain emotion I cannot fully comprehend.

"I'll be outside then," Jonah excuses himself, walking around Exus whose eyes are solely focused on me. Ugh, here we go again.

"I wanted to apologize for what happened. I wasn't trying to make you feel so. . .restricted." He says, offering me an apologetic look.

I stare at his face for a couple of seconds wondering if he is actually serious or not. His emotions look genuine and a sigh rushed out of my mouth.

"I guess it's fine." It wasn't but I was willing to pretend it was if I could get what I want.

"Okay that's great." An enormous smile appearing on his mouth making me uncomfortable. He stares for a few seconds before turning around, making me realize I was to inquire something from him.

"Alpha Exus?" He turns around, eyes growing dim slightly making me realize it's the name, "I want to visit Olivia."

His eyes grow cold almost in an instant, the soft and warm emotions completely disappearing.

"No."

"Why not?" I state quite irritated.

"Olivia is a dangerous person, Ciane and there's no way I am letting my mate go there. Who knows what she'll do or say to you!" He rages, eyes turning dark, his wolf wanting to come out.

"What can she do to me inside a cell, Exus? She cannot attack me inside a silver lined cell right?" I argue.

He's quiet for a few seconds before his eyes narrow, a perplexed look flooding his eyes.

"Wait, why are you so interested in her anyway? Is there something you are not telling me?"

My eyes almost widen at how he has almost caught up with my lies.

"I am interested because another girl is in the same situation I was in a year ago. She's in pain and suffering and I cannot understand if it's real or not. If she deserves it or not." I explain, glaring at him.

"But I have already explained it to you, Ciane. She is not innocent, she killed my niece! She is a killer! You won't visit her!" He exclaims hie voice growing loud.

"And where did you get this information, Exus? Are you sure? Are you absolutely sure that the information is correct!"

"Yes! Yes I am sure! My sister can never lie to me! She would never!" Exus yells almost scaring me to death.

Anabelle is the source of all this information? The same Anabelle who lied to Christian, who rejected Christian and disappeared?

"Okay, fine. I still want to see her."

I can't get through to him. He believes Anabelle and I wanted to believe her too but after realizing all the things she has done, I can't even begin to imagine all the other things she may have done. All the other things she's capable of.

He still looks hesitant and I take a different approach.

"If you want our relationship to work, Exus. Whatever remains of it, it'll have to start here. I cannot live here with you knowing there's a young woman in your cells, a woman who you put there because your sister told you so."

His resolve breaks and sigh leaves his mouth.

"I love my sister, Ciane and I believe her but you are right. I will let you see her. For our relationship." He says before walking away, not waiting for my reply.

A small grin forces itself to my mouth as I turn looking for Jonah. I walk into the living room and spot him in the kitchen, munching some weird fruit.

"Okay, so what's with the smile," he eyes me with confusion.

"Exus agreed! I can visit Olivia."

"Well that's good news!" A small happy chuckle leaving him.

"However, he's a bit suspicious."

"You'll be out of here before he discovers what's happening."

I really hope so. I could not stop the bubbling feeling in my stomach that things would not really go that smoothly.

Chapter 37

"Come on! What are you hiding? Let me see!" Jonah asks trying to peek into the small bag I'm going to smuggle to Olivia.

"It's food and a few girl stuff, Jonah! Unless you are really that curious, you can look." I state as I shove the bag inside the huge jacket I found in the room.

Jonah's face goes bright with embarrassment, "Well you should have started with that!"

"Whatever, come on!" I say, zipping up the jacket and exiting my room.

I quickly race down the stairs almost tripping in the process. Jonah is quick to react and grasp my arm before I roll down the remaining four steps. I offer him a grateful smile easily slipping through his hold and racing to the door.

It only takes a couple of minutes before we are outside the cells. The guard from before bows slightly and let us through not even asking any questions.

"Slow down, Ciane. We'll get there." Jonah grumbles as I rush down the fleet of stairs.

A few seconds later I am standing outside her cell. I see her curled up in a corner, her back to me once more, showing in graphic details the harshness and animosity this pack has. Most of them however have healed, leaving in it's wake scars that will never fully fade.

"Well, hello again Exus's mate." Olivia groans, struggling to stand up. Her eyes fall on Jonah and they soften, her eyes almost filling with tears.

"Jonah," she whispers, her tone completely different from the one she used before.

"Hi, darling, how are you?" He whispers, emotions portrayed on those words.

"Well, same old same old." She grins, "What are you doing here with her?" Her eyes fall on me.

"Your brother sent me."

Her eyes widen, tears gathering in them, finally showing the real pain she's feeling. I could almost feel her grief, the torture she has endured in that cell.

"Christian." She whispers.

"That ring you gave Jonah led him to Christian. I was with him the entire time."

Olivia's brows furrows in confusion, before she speaks again "How did you meet Christian?"

Almost in an instant, the memory surfaces, the rabid wolf that had attacked me leaving me for the dead. The loud boots and the chilling black eyes that stared straight to my soul. And the most prominent feature being his scar. The jagged scar that ran across his face.

"When I ran away I was attacked by a rogue a few miles from here. I had no fighting skills and I was completely defenseless. The rogue tore into me almost killing me. Christian came and saved me." I grin at the memory not actually disgusted by it now, "I never asked why he was so close to this pack then."

A whimper leaves Olivia and my eyes goes to meet hers, "He must have been looking for me. Of a way to get into the pack."

I sigh, unzipping the large coat I had on and pulling out the small bag.

"I brought you some food and other few items." I say as I pass the bag through the bars avoiding the silver.

"Thankyou," she grabs the bag and pulls out an apple, quickly munching on it.

"How did you end up in here, Olivia?" Jonah whispers. Had he asked her this question before?

"Why? What did Exus tell you? Or that bitch, Anabelle." She growls, her eyes flashing dangerously, giving a glimpse of the powerful wolf within.

"He made some accusations but Christian shared some of the things with me."

"What exactly did he tell you?" Olivia asks, looking skeptical about all this. I would be too.

"Well, for starters he was mated to Anabelle. Who was very weird throughout their mateship. He was too hurt to explain the rest." Emotions race through her eyes before a loud sigh escapes her mouth.

"It's quite long story actually." She says, sitting on the dirty floor that almost resembles how she looks.

"When Christian met Anabelle, he was almost in an instant in love with her. He had been waiting for his mate for a while and he marveled at the thought of finding that one person meant for you. When they did meet, it was utter bliss. My parents liked her and it was all going so well. I did not seem to share their thoughts though. I always thought there was something off about her and I did bring the topic up with Christian but he thought I was being paranoid." Her voice breaks slightly.

"Anabelle was so weird that time. She would go missing and I confronted her for it. I asked her where she would go and she woul get so mad. Get violent even. I was scared and Christian wasn't listening to me."

"She knew no one believed me and she made it clear she'd hurt Christian if things don't go her way. So I let her be, knowing there was no way he would hurt he mate. I was wrong. This continued for a while and one day she just. . . disappeared after Christian wanted to mark her. She told Christian she wanted to visit Exus for a while. I remember Christian being so very devastated by it all, but he agreed nonetheless."

"She was gone for a week and when she came back, it was like she was a complete different person. Her grin was bright but her eyes spoke a different story. She apologized for her weird behavior, stating she had been scared and I was even more weirded out. She promised to try and be the best mate for Christian, if he let her visit her brother everyday. Christian was just happy she was back and he obliged. My parents were weary of her after the things she had put Christian through but they let it be. They were mates after all, destined to be together; nothing could come between that. I wish they had."

"It had only been a week when I saw her sneaking into the woods in the middle of the night. It happened a couple of times before I had the courage to follow, hiding my scent completely. It was then that I realized something was very wrong. Anabelle lead me to the deepest parts of our forest to the southern border. All our pack patrol laid on the ground, the smell of wolfsbane emanating from every part of the pack. What even shocked me further was Alpha Exus right there with Anabelle, looking livid."

"I could easily recognize the hunters standing right next to him, holding silver weapons and liquid wolfsbane. Anabelle was already hugging his brother who looked so out of it."

Olivia.

Five years ago.

"Are you sure you want to do this." Exus asked, his eyes scanning Anabelle's ugly face. What does he me- My eyes widen. They are going to attack the pack. Why?

"Yes, Christian has hurt me too much. This pack has hurt me too much! I can no longer bare it. His pack hates me! No one cares for me here, Exus!" Anabelle wails, tears gathering in her eyes, slipping down her cheeks. I almost face palm at how fake she looks. Surely, he doesn't believe her. I await his reply.

"I told you to come home Anabelle! I told you so many times to let me teach him a lesson! You cannot go through this and not let me visit him." Exus mutters, his anger barely intact.

He actually believes her.

"And I have told you, brother. They will feed you lies so you can go against me! Please this is the best option! Destroy them!" Anabelle, says getting evidently irritated.

How can no one tell she is an actual pathological liar?

"Are you sure this pack has caused you so much harm that it needs to be demolished? The hunters are a bit much." The man looks unsure.

He should be! That girl is a complete nutcase.

"Are we taking this pack down or are you going to keep having this stupid conversation?" A hunter, dress impeccably utters eyeing the two with unconcealed distaste. A growl leaves Exus mouth shutting the man and forcing him to bow.

Anabelle stares at his brother, a wicked look shining in her eyes.

"Exus, I. . .I did not want to tell you this but. . .I was pregnant." She utters.

I take a step back in shock, only for me to trip and completely expose myself. All eyes snap to meet mine and an irritated look rushes through Anabelle's eyes.

"What. . . are you doing here?" Anabelle glares, a stutter not concealed, the aim of it not noted. Her grin appears only seconds after. I don't get to stand up before two muscular hunters are drag me where Exus and Anabelle are. I'm dropped in front of them, my knees scrapping on the rough ground.

"What do you mean. . .were?" Exus says, not acknowledging my presence.

A funny emotion races through Anabelle's eyes, too subtle to be notice, before she explains. "She is . . . Christian's sister. The one who has been hurting me. I never told you I was because. . .she threatened to kill my child, my daughter. Your niece."

I'm beyond shocked. Don't tell me he believes this story full of plot holes. Why would I kill my own niece too? Is he using his brain?

"She added wolfsbane to my food. . .and I lost it!" Yeah you've also absolutely lost your mind.

A cackle leaves my mouth as I stare at the devil's incarnate. She has really gone mad. Exus eyes meet mine and the fury in them almost makes me plummet to the floor once more.

"Is this true?" He screams, his eyes shifting dark. In a second his hand is grasping my throat, my feet dangling. He doesn't take regard to my fragile body or the fact that I'm basically a child. I am fourteen years! Why would I even hurt my brother's mate? A nineteen year old female?

"Are you using your tiny brain?" I wheeze as he tightens his hands around my throat further, blocking oxygen from my pathway.

"I am fourteen! Why would I hurt my brother's mate?" I struggle with the words glaring, appalled and astounded by the fact that he believes her or the fact that I'd kill a baby. Has she even ever been pregnant?

His grip falters, eyes widening.

"I told you, Exus. She'll deny it! I am your sister! I would never lie to you!" She exclaims grabbing him by the arm. He lets me go and I drop to the floor, swiftly taking in oxygen through my mouth.

"She was my niece too!"

"Exus please, I cannot move on if I don't do this!" Anabelle states.

The moving on is after demolishing our entire pack.

"Is that the only reason for wanting to kill of all my pack members?" I inquire, already knowing my fate with the hunters standing guard.

"Shut up!" Anabelle screams and snacks me in the face before I can react. I only chuckle and stare at a confused Exus.

"This. . .this is the person you are killing an entire pack for?" I chuckle without humor.

"You have no idea what my sister has been through! You have no right to judge her!" He exclaims, his wolf flashing through his eyes. He walks over to me once more, crouching down and rubbing my now redden cheek.

"I'm not going to kill you. Christian has hurt my sister. You have caused her to lose her child. I will hurt you for my sister." Exus states, beckoning a hunter who brings with him a syringe. Before I can react or move, Exus plunges the needle into my neck consuming me in pure pain. My mindlink shuts off, my form seizing on the floor.

"Your brother defiles my sister, r*pes her and uses her as a toy. What would he do if I did the same to you?" My stomach drops, the pain doubling as I fall completely unconscious.

When I come to, I am laying, thank goddess, complete clothed in my pack. Our pack house. The pack looks broken and shattered. I am laying in my side and something else was missing. I could feel a hollow gap in my chest! I gasp! No no no no. They are gone. My parents are gone.

Tears of pure sorrow gather in my eyes as I race down the stairs in search of them. They can't be gone! I hurry to their room and the sight of my brother shedding tears over the corpse of my parents manages to shake me to the core. The scent of liquid silver and wolfsbane very prominent in the air. They were poisoned.

My pack was okay a few hours ago. It was thriving with children roaming through the pack, Families having fun. My parents alive. Now? Now everything is in disarray. Everyone's gone! Are there survivors? Why? Why hunters? With the amount they were, I doubt there are any left. A hollow feeling grasps my chest as I feel a few more people die. I feel them disconnect from the link and the connection we usually have.

"Christian?" I whisper as I rush to my brother. The brother who looks too broken, too haunted.

"Olivia," he gasps and immediately pulls me in a hug, his scent mixed with blood barely giving me any comfort, "Don't look." I had already though.

The hug doesn't last before the door to the room is pushed open and they both walk in covered in blood. My pack's blood. Pure and adulterated rage rushes through every nerve in my body as I take in the smug looks on Anabelle's face. Why? Why massacre our pack? Why break us? Christian had been nothing but loving, caring and patient with her.

Christian face breaks into an unrecognizable emotion as his eyes flicker between the two.

"Why?" He utters and the same question flows through my mind.

Exus growls fills the room before he is next to Christian and I in an instant, "You dare ask why? After all the things you have put my sister through! All the abuse? The rape! Yes, she told me everything! How you force yourself on her every night! There's no point denying it!" He rages and I stare at him in utter shock.

Really? He believes the bitch. Of course he would!

"Rape? Abuse? What are you talking about?" Christian, my innocent brother looks so clueless that a sharp pain pierces my heart. He has been nothing but good and loving to Anabelle.

Exus does not offer a respond, instead he launches himself at him, punching him on his jaw so hard, he stumbles back as I drop to the floor. I stare in pure fear as he repeats the process over and over again, punching and cursing at him.

"Stop! Stop!" I find myself yelling for the beast of a man. He trusts the sister and he's killing my brother.

With a rush of adrenaline I quickly get off the floor and hit Exus's back. He lets go momentarily eyes shifting to me. The rage, malice and pure chaos in his eyes makes me stumble back in terror. He raises his fist and I close my eyes waiting for the impact on my face. It never comes. Instead, a wicked emotion flashes through his eyes. He turns back to my near unconscious brother and pulls out a silver knife and my stomach drops.

"Anabelle, you should do the honours. He was your mate after all." He grins and offers it to an eager Anabelle. Are they okay? Are they insane?

I rush to shield him but Exus is too quick to prevent me from doing so. I watch in pure anguish as Anabelle grabs Christian'd face on her palm and tears through his skin creating a messy pattern. A loud cry escapes his mouth and I watch in horror, tears rushing down my eyes. He doesn't deserve this! I can't even help him. My brother! I elbow the beast holding me and he doesn't even move. How can a fourteen years old beat up a gigantic monster?

"You're just getting what you deserve, love." Anabelle taunts, as blood gushes through the wound that's barely healing.

"You ruined my sister! I'm taking yours, Christian and there's nothing you can do to stop me!" Exus mocks as his arms tighten around me. I see Christian struggle, his eyes shutting almost losing his consciousness.

"No. . .no. . .please don't! A-anyone but my sister!" He begs and I don't even try to stop my tears. I don't even try to control how I'm breaking from within. My strong brother begging a monster to let me go. The brother who had been loving to his pathetic mate, the same brother who has been there for me from the beginning, the brother who is now laying down, bleeding and scarred in so many ways. Why him? Why me? Why us?

I sob as I watch him lose consciousness, his eyes shutting off completely.

"Shouldn't we just finish him off?" Anabelle offers and my eyes widen in pure horror. Does she not feel anything for the mate she has been with? How apathetic is she? How insane is she?

"No, this will suffice. We have broken him. He has no pack and his sister will be long gone when he wakes up." Exus concludes, have a voice holding no emotions.

His hands that had been grasping my waist, suddenly let's go and I don't even hesitate to give him a hot slap to the cheek.

"You have murdered everyone! You killed my parents! My pack! What is wrong with you people?" I scream, the raw emotion shaking my entire body. Everyone I've ever loved, gone. I have no one. Are there any survivors?

I'm too hurt and too emotional to notice the syringe heading to my neck until it's plunged deeply. It only takes a few second for the wolfsbane to take action and a scream rips out of my mouth as agonizing pain floods my body from the dangerous substance coursing through my blood stream.

"One day I will get vengeance for my people, Exus! I promise you that." It is the last words I utter before everything begins to blur. I manage to meet Anabelle's eyes and note the pure elation and satisfied looks that run through her eyes.

"When I woke up, I was here. Cold and in pain. I had just lost my pack, my family and there was no one! No one to tell me it would be okay! Everything was so wrong! I couldn't escape. I tried so many times until I just gave up. Where would I go anyways, I had no one. I wasn't sure Christian was even alive at all. Were there any survivors?" She explains and my mouth hangs open.

Exus and Anabelle. How animalistic can they get? Massacring an entire pack just because Anabelle claimed she was abused. And that Olivia killed her baby? Was he even using that brain of his? What sort of alpha does not investigate the matter? What sort of alpha hires hunters to murder an entire pack?

Because he knew!

He knew no one would support his ideas without any good reason for it. Without investigating all those claims made by the sister. Yet he did not! He acted irrationally with no consideration for the pack.

What sort of man kidnaps a fourteen years old girl and locks her up for five years because his much 'mature' sister said so? More important, what sort of person makes such preposterous accusations and why?

Tears of anguish flood my eyes. She has gone through so much and she looks so strong! So very strong. An 'I am so sorry' will not do in this case. Nothing will. She watched her family get murdered, her brother get scarred, her entire pack get destroyed. If I hated Exus before, right now I completely loathed him.

"You deserve so much better, my love." My eyes fall to Jonah who looks almost just as shattered as Olivia. The emotions on his face portraying all his feelings. Tears begin to stream down her eyes and I have to look away. I thought my story was horrible, I thought mine was messed up. Who knew how many people Exus could scar in his lifetime.

"We need to get you out of here!" I murmur, quickly wiping the tears out of my eyes.

Before I can decide on what to do next, a familiar cackle stops me in my tracks. My eyes glances to the stairs and my eyes meet with hers. The woman who has caused enough suffering to everyone, the woman who has found pure pleasure in the tears of others. The woman whose eyes are as dark as the darkness.

"I knew you were here for a reason, omega. Too bad you're not getting out of here alive. None of you are."

Chapter 38

I glare at the woman staring at me with a dark glint and a psychotic look in her eyes. The rage I feel is so deep, I feel the sprouting of fur just below my skin begging to come to the surface to deal with the inhumane woman. A woman who has caused feuds and thrived by it. She has caused so much hurt to not only me but also the entirety of Olivia's pack.

"You bitch! How dare you! How dare you!" Those words leave my mouth, the rage and anger portrayed in detail.

"Do you feel hurt that I destroyed her pack or that I turned everyone against you? Have you ever thought why. Why everyone disliked you? It was all me. I broke you! I broke you!" The laugh that leaves her mouth leaves me in utter shock.

I stare at Jonah who looks too stunned and confused at the same type. I don think he's ever seen Anabelle so unhinged and completely lost to reality.

"Well looks like a mental hospital it is." Olivia mutters as we all watch as she races down the stairs towards us.

"Did it hurt when I brought your pack to it's knees? I know it did! Tell me it did!" A giggle leaves her mouth as she gets closer to us. Jonah goes into protective mode and a snarl leaves his mouth. Anabelle's eyes meet Jonah's and I realize, she's not really there. She hasn't been for a while now.

"Christian was so naive thinking that I'd just be with him. That I'll stick around and be a Luna! How pathetic and stupid he was to have believed all my lies! All the things I told him! I mean why didn't he follow it up! Because he trusted me! He trusted me and I utilized it!" Her eyes grow blank and she's quiet for a while. Without warning a cackle escapes her mouth giving me a fright. She has lost it.

She gets closer to us, her voice growing unreasonably loud. What the freak is wrong with her? Her eye look wild, crazy even.

"I am going to kill you! I am going to finish what I started and nothing, nothing you say will stop me from--" she suddenly goes quiet, her eyes widening for a second before her entire body goes still, eyes shutting as she drops to the floor, revealing a familiar man behind her.

"Ashton?" Jonah whispers, staring at the man as if he has grown another set of eyes.

"She talks too much," he grins, displaying an array of pearly te eth."Now hurry, we have no time! The drug will not last long." He fumbles through his pocket and pulls a set of keys.

"What?" I stare in complete shock. What is going on?

He rushes to the cell holding Olivia and unlocks it, hissing in the process. I'm still too in shock to understand what's going on. Why is he helping us?

"Why are you helping?"Olivia asks the very question that was about to leave my lips.

"Christian."

My mind flashes back to the time the man had insisted we could come up with another plan. He already had a spy already. When did he get here? How did he know about me working for Christian?

"How?" I ask, completely perplexed by the entire situation.

"I've been here for over a year now. Christian had been looking for a way to get into the pack. He knew the only way to get in was to place someone in this pack who will get all the information out of here. It was at that time Christian found you, Ciane. He brought you in and nursed all your wounds. Weirdly enough, he didn't even bother to ask why we found you not too far away from this pack." Ashton explains and everything makes alot more sense.

"You have been here the whole time and you did not bother to look for me?" I glance at Olivia who looks enraged.

"We can have this conversation when we are out of this pack. Right now, it's crucial that we escape." Ashton says as Jonah helps Olivia exit the cell she has occupied for the last five years.

We hurry up the stairs and pass a knocked out guard on the way. There are still so many unanswered questions. How did the communicate? How did no one realize that a mole existed in this pack?

I could hear Olivia's breath getting rugged as we rushed towards the border of the pack. The fact that no one has followed us this far is alarming and weird. Was Anabelle still unconscious?

"Stop! What are you doing close to the border?" An unfamiliar voice demands and I turn to stare at one of the border patrol. He looks about my age, a scowl occupying his features.

"Its okay, Evan. I'm in charge here. The alpha knows we are here and it would be best if you just move aside." Jonah commanded and Evan's eyes widen before he bows and moves aside.

It was going so smoothly until the said alpha himself emerges through the thick trees, a livid expression marring his features.

"Where do you think you're going with her?" Exus snarls, his mouth baring his sharp canines. His eyes meet mine and a hurt expression forms on his face.

"I knew you insisting to see her was weird but I didn't think you'd try to break her out. Anabelle was right, wasn't she?" He mumbles and I am almost sure I see tears gather in his eyes.

His eyes fog over and a few minutes later we are surrounded by pack wolves, most of them in their wolf form.

"I know everything now, Exus. You attacked Olivia's Pack and massacred everyone just because you trusted your sister too much to investigate her accusations!" I glare and his eyes widen, fear and shame clouding them before they harden.

"My sister would never lie to me. She would never do anything to cause harm to a another pack. His pathetic brother destroyed my sister's life and she, she killed my niece." He still goes by the same narrative five years later. Had he never bothered to investigate his sister's claims?

"Are you absolutely sure her accusations were true, accurate?" Jonah asks and Exus looks utterly betrayed.

"Jonah why would you side with her? Ashton? You can't possibly believe all the lies she's told you?" Exus mutters, with disbelieving eyes.

"You are actually the one who's in the dark. You've fought battles for someone who will never do the same for you! You have destroyed an entire pack because of something so trivial that your sister made up, that your sister fabricated in order to make you compliant with her disgusting plans!" Ashton seethes through clenched teeth and I can feel the pain in his voice as if he went through it himself, as if he had seen it happen.

It hits me like a tidal wave.

He was part of Christian's pack.

Exus opens his mouth to retort but before he does, an enraged Anabelle stumbles right behind him, her eyes wild and unstable. Any signs of humanity left in them completely gone.

"What are you doing here?" Exus asks turning to stare at her, his brows furrowing in confusion.

"I'm here to witness it all end. What I started must come to a wonderful end, right?" Annabelle chuckles, as he always and bounces slightly on her foot.

"What are you talking about, Anabelle?"

"Oh, drop the act brother! I know you must have loved destroying that stupid pack like I did. Tell me that you did! I won't judge you! I would embrace you because I did too! You remember the blood, the way I broke Christian's little heart? It was all so satisfyingly hilarious." She screeches as she sways in circles.

Exus eyes widen with fear, confusion and alot of other emotions I couldn't decipher.

"What... What do you mean?" He sounds afraid.

"Did you really think Christian had the guts to hurt me? He was such a weakling! He was so smitten by our bond, by me, gave me everything I wanted, all the freedom in the world! That man was so blind! He trusted me and you did too! You did too! You were so stupid, brother!" She grins and Exus looks haunted, "Don't worry brother! I know you loved it! You loved the blood! You loved it when we brought that pack down to it's knees!" She mumbles rubbing her eyes wildly ad her eyes meet mine.

I flinch when I realize her eyes are vacant. No signs of life or humanity in them. There's always a glimpse of someone through their eyes, the light that shows that some where behind their twisted self is a soul, a mind and someones child. Hers are blank and I stumble back at the look.

"Annabelle, we. . .we destroyed an entire pack for. . .nothing?" Exus asks, eyes solely focused on the woman who's eyes are on mine.

"Don't feel bad brother, they meant nothing. It was so easy to convince you that you had a niece, that that disgusting little fourteen year old had killed her. It was so worth it to see the defeated look on their faces as I took them down as I destroyed every little thing they held dear to their heart. Soon I'll be destroying the remaining ones." She grins and I turn my eyes to Exus. He looks sick, repulsed by what he has heard. But I know deep down he must have felt it, that the attack was all for nothing. He must have known that one of them must ha been lying and he chose to believe the sister, the liar, the mastermind behind everything.

My eyes turn to stare at the guards who were with Exus. Their expression mirror Exus's but with disgust in the mix. They can't believe their alpha is so monstrous, ready to annihilate a pack based on words of an unstable woman.

"You destroyed us, Exus! You and your sister have hurt us beyond repair!" Olivia speaks up,

I witness as Exus's eyes harden as his stares train on us. It's like he was done with it all.

"It doesn't matter anymore, does it. Your pack is gone and there's nothing to be done to take back what has happened." Exus replies his eyes gazing into mine.

It only takes a second for me to realize he has chosen his sister. The sister that destroyed an entire pack. He may as well have known from the beginning.

"And I thought you'd be a bit remorseful about it, Exus." I mutter, his name finally slipping through my lips.

Exus green eyes widen for a second before the grow cold and empty. The emptiness I had witnessed so very many times, when he detaches himself from reality.

"Guards, attack them!" Exus yells and I witness as them divide. Half of them takes Exus sides, the others heading our direction. Why were they choosing us? Why were they choosing to betray Exus. Exus, the man who has proven more than once that he's not a nice guy. Noticing this, Exus eyes burn with rage.

"You dare disobey my order! You will face my wrath, you'll face the consequences of your actions." His eyes shift into that dark color I am so used to.

I am in shock and I swallow hard, staring as his claws elongate, canines protruding from his teeth. I have never seen him too un-hinged. He has chosen to listen to his sister, he has chosen her and I am not shocked or surprised. Even when she has proven so many times that she's a killer, a murderer, he has chosen her.

"I knew you'd choose me, brother!" Anabelle cackles as her claws emerge from her fisted hand.

I sense him before I see him and every cell in my body comes alive as if he was entwined with me which is literally impossible. He emerges through the trees and I swallow hard as his dark eyes meet mine, the scar on his face becoming even more prominent than ever. I witness as Anabelle's eyes widen with shock before they turn dark and lifeless, a smirk so dark and daunting curling at the corner of her lips. She stares at the man that used to her her mate with both hunger and rage. A confusing mix.

"Have you come to die, mate?"

Chapter 39

I made contact with his eyes and I watch as they soften. They shift from mine and fall on the female right next to me and his breath hitches. Even from the distance, I can see the tears gathering in his eyes, various emotions rushing through his eyes. The pain, the love, the remorse and the vengeance, all merged together into one. It was his sister after all. A sister he has not seen for five long, torturous years because of his horrible mate. I could see what those years had done to him and how he had been cold and so detached.

"This fight is long overdue. Exus you murdered my entire pack without remorse, with no consideration for anyone but your own self." Christian states, as he stares at Exus completely disregarding Anabelle and her comment.

He no longer felt anything for her, I noted. They had been bonded, almost mated for life and now, now they were enemies, completely and utterly against each other.

There's utter silence for a few seconds before everything breaks loose. The guards shift attacking the ones that had shifted to our side. My eyes wide at the abrupt change that just occurred. I watch wide eyed as Olivia stumbles to the floor, Jonah acting as his protection. Exus shifts mid air attacking Christian who only grins, the smile looking utterly scary and horrid on his face. I knew at that instant Christian has been waiting for this encounter for a very long time. To finally serve out justice for every member that has died or suffered and I was all in for it.

Before I can react to help Olivia up, something or someone drags me by my hair, painfully so.

"You bitch, this is all your fault! You brought this upon us! If you hadn't ran away like the coward you are we wouldn't be here! You should have faced your death with honour, you imbecile!" Her screechy voice screams near my ear almost deafening me.

I could feel her dragging me by my hair, almost detaching them from my scalp. I knew she wasn't going to stop so with so much strength, I move closer to her, before slamming my elbow on her stomach, making her lose her breath and I am able to detach myself from her.

I turn around and deliver a quick punch to her face, a whimper rushing out of her mouth as she falls to the ground with a thud.

"No, this is your fault! You destroyed a pack with no remorse! It was you and I'm going to love beating that disgusting face of yours." I grin, and rage floods her eyes, the unhinged look coming back to play. She quickly rises up, her green eyes glaring at me with so much loathe in them.

I stare at her and watch as her hand folds forming a fist and she goes to punch me. I sidestep and angle my body away from her to the right and she goes stumbling. She does it again and again and I keep moving, avoiding her hits as they get sloppier.

"Stand still so I can hit you, you pathetic bitch!" She hisses as she tries once again and completely fails. It comes to my attention that she has completely gone insane. It has been happening slowly and now she was at it's peek.

"What's wrong Anabelle, are you finally going crazy?" I taunt as I watch her green eyes shift black, her wolf coming out to dance. She was growing impatient as her long claws protrude from her fingertips.

She swings her arms and completely misses me, swiping her feet to the left, I move to the right only for her to move quickly and deliver a very precise blow to my nose, instantly causing my nose to bleed. A grin forms on her mouth and I watch as she tries to do the love again only I'm wiser than that.

My eyes unconsciously shift to Christian whose movement are fluid and completely composed as he attacks a shifted Exus. Alphas fighting each other. As enchanting as it is, I knew it's dangerous to take my eyes off an enemy who wants me dead.

I move aside just as Anabelle goes to punch me once again. She is getting worse and I am enjoying every bit of it.

"Do you really know how your parents really died, Ciane?" That completely captures my attention and she realizes this.

"I mean you are just a naive little girl, aren't you?" She taunts her eyes meeting mine.

"What do you know about my parents?" I rage, my eyes shifting color, my wolf's eyes.

"Ah I have your attention now. My parents they loved power, they were enchanted by it, couldn't get enough of it. As one of the strongest pack my father wasn't satisfied so he planned on getting more territory by attacking smaller packs close to us and as his most trusted men, a strong warrior and ally, your father was part of father's council. They helped and advised him. When he brought the topic up, your father was horrified by it and warned him not to take that action. My father thought he was jesting and soon would change his mind. He didn't. A few weeks after, the werewolf council came and my father was arrested and taken for questioning and if he will ever consider attacking a pack. It took years for my father to build his reputation. During that time, your father thrived and my father's hate for him grew double fold. My father plotted to get rid of your father but your mother couldn't leave his side even for a second so he had to do what must be done." Anabelle cruelly relates the fate my wonderful parents suffered.

"So they weren't killed by hunters?" I stutter the words too unbelievable and too scary for me go to even imagine.

A chuckle, cold and menacing, emanates from her mouth and my eyes water, "Of course they were but also not, they were just pathetic wolves who wanted to do the right thing. Too bad your mother had to be caught up in the mix. Samira was an amazing woman." She mocks and rage instantly floods my being.

It was the first time my mother's name was being mentioned after so very many years and yet I still had questions.

"How did you know your father did that?" I couldn't say the words.

"You mean kill your parents?" She chuckles-cakles and both anger and grief floods my chest, almost knocking the breath out of me."You don't have any idea what nonsense things alphas record down."

It suddenly makes sense.

"That's why you easily accessed the hunters because your father had access to them to kill my family."

"We have a winner!" She cackles as she spin around, her giggles filling the battle field.

I could feel all emotions coursing through me and yet I couldn't seem to grasp any of them. My parents had been murdered by the same people that murdered Christian's parents. My mate rejected me just like the way Christian did. My mate scarred my face just like the way Christian's did. How poetic that truly is.

"So are you going to enact your justice oh, Ciane?"

I want to, I really want to but Christian's voice suddenly floods my head as his words come back. Emotions, either anger or grief clouds ones judgement. I couldn't attack her because although I'm not physically vulnerable, emotionally I totally am. However, I wasn't going to let her leave unscathed.

"Come at me, bitch!"

"That's what I like to hear."

And so our dance begin.

She runs towards me, her feet moving quite fast reminding me she's also a warrior. I deliver several punches and she does too, most of them missing my face. She does a complicated move and I find myself face planting to the floor.

Rage floods my mind and I quickly get up, ready. The fight was taking too long and completely making me mad. I deliver a brutal punch to her face and hear her bone crush. I don't give her time to recover before I'm punching her lower side of her stomach, aiming for her ribs. I hear a crack and a wail escapes her mouth. She is losing it, I could see it now. Her eyes were always looking lost and a new foreign thing occupied them. Something cold and unhinged.

She tries to grab my hair once more but I quickly slip through her hold, giving me access to her unprotected body. I brutally punch the other side of her stomach and she finally plummets to the floor, unconscious. That was quite fast.

My eyes finally shift from her to Christian and Exus. My eyes solely focus on Christian, fear for his life and awe at his fighting skills. It's at that moment that I realize Exus is no match for Christian. Exus had not anticipated that the pack he had destroyed a few years ago would be back here, destroying what he loves. Christian looks collected as he flings Exus away by the scruff of his neck. Even from the distance I am at, I hear his whimper. Christian isn't shifted and he's able to completely attack Exus, and brutally at that.

My eyes move to Olivia whose being protected by one guard and Jonah. I stare as one of the guards detaches a wolf's neck from their body. Brutal. My eyes move back to Exus who is about to attack Christian again. His eyes shift to meet mine and they widen considerably. He completely disregards Christian and races towards me. Christian looks towards me too and he has the same reaction.

"Ciane, watch out!" It's yelled.

I knew then my mistake before it even happened.

I had turned my back on an enemy.

I try to turn around only for me to hit the floor as a wolf's body rams itself on me, taking the blow that was supposed to be mine from the cold hearted woman behind me as we both fall down to the grassy field. The dark brown wolf, whimpers on top of me as the crimson liquid touch my hands. I stare at the wolf as it shifts to it's human form. I drag myself away as the blood coats my clothes, the metallic scent flooding my nose.

"No! What have you done! What have you done!" The wicked witch wails, now realizing the error of her deeds.

I stare at the silver knife embedded deep in his chest, the handle being the only visible part. The scent hits me almost in an instant, and the glittery purple powder coating the silver blade evident. Wolfsbane. My eyes widen as they meet the horrified ones of Anabelle.

"That knife was for you, you pathetic bitch but he just had to run and try to stop me! He had to try and stop the inevitable! No! No! No!" She screeches.

"I am going to kill you, I am going to dest-" She doesn't finish her sentence before she plummets to the floor, someone hitting her from behind. I don't pay attention to them as I regard the man whose on the floor.

Exus stares up at me, his eyes glazing over with emotions I don't understand. His body is ridden with new fresh scars that shows he's quite a sloppy warrior and a terrible alpha at that. The recent encounter with Christian making them even worse. I stare down at him and for the first time, I feel sorry for him. Sorry because he has been horrible all his life, sorry that he destroyed his own life for revenge, and sorry for everyone that has ever encountered him.

The blade is too deep, I note. Even the flesh around the blade begins to sizzle emitting a weird scent, burning my nose. The battle had come to a stand still, the alpha responsible for it all having fallen. With no leader, the remaining ones stranded and completely lost.

"Ciane, mate!" He slurs as he tries to hold my hand. I let him. The spark instantly ignites on my hand and his smile widen bringing to display his blood coated teeth.

He's not going to make it.

"I'm so sorry. I'm sorry for what I did to you. I'm sorry I hurt you instead of protecting you, I destroyed our bond before I even knew it existed." He stutters and my eyes flood with tears. I didn't know why. I have never cared for him and that particular moment I am absolutely sure that I feel nothing for him and yet, I couldn't help the tears.

I stare at the blade deep in his chest and look up to meet his eyes.

"Don't cry," he chuckles before they turn into coughs,"I don't deserve your tears, I don't deserve anything. We were never going to be together, I knew that but I just wanted to hold onto that hope, that maybe we would. You'd never love me, I saw it in your eyes. There was nothing but resentment and I deserve it all."

I could see his eyes flickering, his breath growing slow and almost too shallow.

"I don't deserve your forgiveness, I do not. I feel it you know, I can feel the blade. It's too deep so please. Please just lie to me, lie to me that you forgive me. I don't want to go knowing that you hate me. Just..." He coughs, his eyes flooding with tears, "Just lie to me, Ciane. Tell me you forgive me. My actions are unredeemable. I have created chaos for so many people. So...just lie."

He grips my hand almost too painfully but I offer no reaction. I look up and my eyes meets Christian who has a few bruises on his face already healing. His face is void of emotions and yet deep in there I can see the rage, anger, relief and grief swimming within. Right next to him stands Jonah who looks completely heartbroken and shattered. Olivia on the other hand looks almost elated by the suffering displayed on Exus face. I don't blame her, he deserves worse. Exus was finally paying, even though shortly, for what he has done to her.

"Please. . .lie to me." He whimpers, as he gurgles, the blood finally dripping down his nose.

When I came here I didn't think he'd be dead. I wanted justice to prevail. For both of them to suffer for what they have done, to both Christian and me. For his pack, for Olivia, for everyone who has received and suffered at his hands Both of these monsters who have done so much harm it's too much to handle. He didn't deserve to die so quickly, he didn't deserve to go so easily but yet, he had taken the blade for me, he had protected me from my own demise. Did that count for something?

Every pain and every suffering that I have ever encountered in my life by his hands rushes through my mind, every emotion he has made me go through storms my mind and yet at that moment, peace floods me. He deserves worse and I deserve so much better.

"I forgive you." I utter and a grin forms on his mouth. His eyes shift to Christian and Olivia and emotions flood his eyes before he shuts them. He shift to Jonah and I hear him mumble a few words. I don't dwell on them.

I witness, with my own eyes, as his pupils dilate as he takes a final breath before it exits from his mouth, eyes growing cold.

It happens.

I feel the tearing of our bond, the pain accompanying as whatever goddess given bond becomes shattered pieces. And yet, I still feel nothing. No pain of his lose, no remorse yet tears flood down my eyes. I know I don't love him, never even considered it, but I couldn't stop crying.

My eyes move and I meet an unconscious Anabelle being held down by Ashton. Anabelle the perpetrator of all the things happening. It only takes a few seconds for howls to break out as they sense the death of their alpha, their leader. It's nothing to me, really. I look up and meet Christian's eyes and they are filled with so much emotions I almost break down once again.

Exus is dead. That fact would take a while getting used to. He didn't suffer like how I had envisioned it, dreamt of it.

He just smoothly sailed away to save me. I don't know how to feel about that.

Chapter 40

I stare out the window, emotions flooding my chest. Exus was dead and yet, I still felt hollow. Punishing Exus for what he had done to me had been what drove my life. It had been the only thing that had pushed my life. Before the anger and the thirst for revenge, what had drove me was survival. How to survive a new day, how to hide from Exus. I have spent my life not knowing what I wanted to do because I had never thought beyond Exus. He was always there, hiding in the shadows hunting me, in my memories and nightmares, terrorizing me. Now that he is gone, I'm lost, completely clueless on what to do. What is driving me now?

It has only been a few weeks since his death and the council, the bastards, were called because an alpha has just died. The old men claimed they had paid Exus to investigate the massacre at Christian's pack a five years ago and him being the murderer, he had come up with an enticing tale about the hunters. None of them had bothered to investigate further. Totally their fault.

"What are you thinking about?" His voice startles me and I yelp.

"Dude, you don't do that." I glare at Christian as he grins with amusement and comes to stand right next to me. My eyes shift to meet his tall form and I instantly look away. I was painfully aware now of the attraction I had for him. I didn't want to address it or bring it up. Ever.

"Nothing really. Just how strange things have played out."

His emotions shift and I look at the large expanse of trees covering his mansion.

"Anabelle is set to be executed this week." He mumbles and I turn to look at him, trying to gauge his reaction.

"How does that make you feel?" I inquire.

"Indifferent. At one point I might have considered her my mate but now, I honestly don't care what happens to her." Understandably so.

After the council had visited Exus's pack, it had been disbanded, members being free to choose whatever pack they wanted to join. Christian remained without a pack and the council, because of their own negligence, had suggested he rebuilds The Night Star Pack and invite back members if any were willing to come back. They had promised to offer all the resources necessary to rebuild a pack. He hadn't decided on it yet. And I was curious now.

"Do you plan on rebuilding your pack?" I ask and angle my body towards him. He does the same and we are both staring right at each other now.

"I honestly don't know." He whispers, "Do you remember that particular time I came here and was completely beaten up?" He asks.

How could I forget that? It was the first time I realized there was a story there.

"Yes, vaguely." He grins and my heart pounds.

"Well, I had been looking for a way to free my sister, a way into Exus pack and I had never really discovered much. I stumbled upon three of my pack members. They had completely gone rogue, eyes shifted red. I couldn't believe that the people we had been together had gone completely mad, rogue. It was so scary, I just couldn't find the strength to fight back. The people who I was supposed to lead were stranded out there, completely shattered without an alpha. When the pack was demolished I ran. I couldn't face my people. I had let them down as an alpha, as the heir, as the one whose supposed to be there for them through it all. That even made it worse. Without an alpha, there's no pack. I just don't think I want to put them or myself in that situation ever again." I could hear the palpable grief in his voice and that shakes me too."That is why you never knew I was an alpha. It was something I wanted not to be. I just wanted not to feel the shame associated with what had happened." Christian was embracing his grief, I noted.

"I let them hurt me because I deserved it. I deserved it for failing them." He reveals and my heart breaks for him. I never knew he felt this guilty, this bad about it.

Without over thinking it, I grab his hand firmly, "It's not your fault, Christian. It never was. The only people to blame here are Anabelle and Exus. They are the people that ruined your life. They are the ones that destroyed everything. Even if you had been there, there would have been nothin you would have done. Olivia told me everything. She told me how you got your scar and how she was kidnapped. I promise you it wasn't your fault and your pack wouldn't hold it against you. Apart from being an alpha, you're also a brother, someone's child, a human who has emotions. You had just lost your parents and your sister and your pack and you reacted in the best way you knew how to. If someone ever blames you for that, then they are the ones who are at fault." I say it all at once, not even taking a break from the rant.

It seems like so long ago when he was shutting me out and literally insulting me during training. I can't believe it's the same person right here taking to me.

When he becomes to quiet, my eyes shift up to meet his and my breath hitches. I had never seen so many emotions in his eyes before, so many warm emotions that hold me captive that I don't want to look away.

"You know you're so amazing, right." He whispers and my cheeks turn crimson.

"No, please do repeat it again." I chuckle lightly and his lips stretch in a grin, displaying the small dimple I had never noticed on his left cheek.

"You're absolutely wonderful, Ciane. I was so horrible to you, mean and a complete asshole and I am so sorry for that. I don't think there's enough apologies that would make up for my rude behavior. I never even put your emotions into perspective and I never thought about you. I was just too focused on me that I completely disregarded you, for that I apologize." He speaks so sincerely that my eyes widen considerably.

I lift my feet off the ground and touch his forehead with the back of my hand, "Are you sure you're okay. Or your aren't Christian at all."

He smiles, "That guy was horrible."

I find myself smiling back, "I forgive you, Christian. I'm sorry too. I was quite pushy sometimes."

"You're forgiven." He whispers,"There's something else I wanted to ask you."

He's quiet for a while and I nod my head.

"Would you let me kiss you?"

My breath hitches and unconsciously my eyes drop down to his lips, pink and luscious. Hypnotically, I take steps towards him and he does too, completely shattering the space between us.

"Yes." It sounds breathless.

Without any single inhibition, his lips comes crushing down on my mine and I swear I feel sparks. It's nothing I've ever felt before, considering it's my first consensual kiss. His lips move with mine in perfect synchrony, taking my breath completely away. It's perfect, it's just right and I love it.

When we finally pull away my face is red, I can feel it and shyly look away from him, earning a deep chuckle from his chest.

"I really really like you, Ciane." Christian confesses and I stare at him wide eyed.

I care for him, I know I do but at that moment I realize I don't know who I am. I have spent half my life running and hiding who I was. I spent my younger years running from Exus and the previous year wanting revenge for what he had done. I had never discovered who I was. And caring for Christian isn't enough, liking him isn't enough.

Christian must have noticed the hesitation in my eyes because he speaks up.

"This confession is not for you to confess too, Ciane. I'm just saying that I really like you. I just want you to be aware of my feelings for you." He smiles and it's genuine that I find myself telling him.

"I like you too Christian, I really do. I just have no idea who I am right now. I have spent half my life running from Exus, hiding and wanting revenge. I just have no idea who I am right now. I have spent most of my years hiding behind a facade in order to survive. I know I like you but I need to know who I am. It's not a no. I just want to discover who I am first before I decide what's next." I say, knowing it is what it is and there's nothing I can do about it. It wouldn't be fair for him or me to go into this if I am not ready for it.

"I understand Ciane and I just want to let you know that I'll wait for you. However long it takes." He grins and my heart stutters at the tremendous changes he has gone through.

"You really have changed." I whisper as I find myself falling into his arms.

"We both have."

"Hello, love birds!" Olivia's voice pulls me out of his arms so fast I almost stumble to the floor.

"No need to be shy, I saw everything!" She grins and I become red.

"Don't do that!" Christian chuckles and pulls Olivia into a warm hug.

In this past few weeks, Olivia and Christian had become so close, tears had been shedded and a few things broken but they are were now stronger than ever. Christian was still enraged about the decimation of his entire pack and Olivia knowing she had wasted five years, she had been punished and hurt for no reason, for accusations and things that weren't her fault.

"I'm going to leave you two." I smile at Olivia who returns it. We had grown quite close. I had told her my story and she had told me hers. It had been so painful how almost identical our stories were. The abuse we faced and the hurt we had to endure. We bonded over that and shared a few laughs along the way.

Christian grins and I return it.

"The tension here is killing me, guys!" Olivia says with amusement and I hurry away blushing profusely while she cackles behind me.

I stare at Ciane's retreating figure, chuckling at how cute her and my brother are. I turn to Christian and find a silly grin occupying his mouth, a vulnerable look shining in his eyes.

We are both quiet for a few seconds before he speaks up.

"I'm planning on rebuilding our pack. In honour of our parents." Christian's says and my eyes water.

It has been so long since I lost them and yet the memories are so vivid in my mind. They were the most amazing people ever and I just cannot believe they are gone. Taken away from me.

"I think that's a good idea, Christian. Dad would be so proud of that." I whisper and Christian smiles and pulls me to his chest.

"I've missed you so much, Liv." He says and the tears finally falls down my eyes.

"I have missed you too big brother, so much." My voice breaks and his hold tightens.

Ten seconds later, I pull away and punch him harshly on his shoulder.

"Hey," he grumbles and I only grin.

My eyes move and stare at where Ciane just walked through and a question comes to mind.

"Are you going to tell her?" I ask, and his eyes turns a vivid green. His wolf.

"I don't know, maybe eventually. Right now she needs time to herself. She doesn't need to know that my wolf and I have chosen her as my mate. I didn't even know about it until Anabelle tried to kill her." Christian explains, his eyes growing cold, remembering when Ciane almost lost her life, had Exus not sacrificed his for her, and

I get him. It was when Anabelle had raised the dagger ready to kill her did his wolf come to the surface to make the claim. She was his.

It isn't something that happens often but it does happen.

"How long are you going to wait before you tell her."

"As long as it takes."

I grin.

"Good answer."

Epilogue

"**I** find you here everytime. What do you like about this view?" Christian once again manages to startle for the millionth time.

I glare at him as he walks towards me, a smile occupying his lips, "I've told you not to do that."

"You're always so lost in thought. It's funny." He says and I give him a nasty glare. He only chuckles and my anger dissipate. He can be so annoying at times, most times though he's quite charming.

"So do tell what are you thinking about this time. You usually come here when you are in deep thought."

It has been two years, two years since Christian decided to rebuild his pack, since he discovered there were quite a number of survivors from Night Star Pack and they were ready to come back to the pack. A few refused to join back after the massacre opting to stay in the packs they were or remain lone wolves. A few wolves from Exus pack had even wanted to join the pack. I was quite skeptical at first and gave them six months probation. Some left and a few remained in those six months.

Night Star Pack was now growing in number. Christian took train-ing very seriously promising he would never be unprepared like the last time there was an attack. He had proven more than once that he is a capable and wise alpha and everyone trusted his decision.

Two years had changed me too. I didn't realize I had a lot to work on. The emotional and mental trauma left by Exus had been so deep and I had not realized how bad it was.

It took a while for my mental health to be stable and I went to therapy for that. Christian has been supportive ever since he confessed his feelings for me. When I told him I wasn't ready, I expected him to shun me off but he has stood with me all the way.

It had taken two years for me to be ready, ready for a relationship with him. Ready to move forward, ready to leave Exus, Anabelle and Wolf Creek Pack behind me. Here I was, now wanting to tell him that.

"Hey, are you okay?" Christian asks, concern flooding his voice. He takes my hand and I gasp.

No way. I did not just feel sparks.

"What's wrong?"

I stare at him wide eyed.

"You're going to think I'm crazy but..." He nods his head.

"I feel sparks." He stares blankly before realization dawns on him. "Oh."

"You knew." My mouth drops open when he looks guilty.

"Yes, I did. Remember when Anabelle..." His eyes darken before he continues, "My wolf had chosen you long before then and I just realized it at that time. When I accepted the bond, it grew stronger each day."

That means, he's felt this for two years?

"Yes."

"Why didn't you say anything and why am I feeling this now."

"Because I didn't want to take the choice away from you, Ciane. You weren't ready and believe it or not, I wasn't too. We spent our time together plotting revenge and wanting to bring Exus down. At that time we would have been just toxic to each other. And because you didn't know of the bond because you hadn't accepted me then, the bond was dormant. Now. . .I can feel it."

I did too. A small singular thread, attaching me to him that would grow thicker everyday.

"I would wait as long as you want, Ciane." Christian says and I smile.

"I think, no, I know I am ready now. There's nothing holding me back." A smile forms on his mouth as he pulls me for a long hug.

When he pulls away, he stares at me with an indecipherable look and I blush.

"Have I ever told you why our pack is named Night Star?" He asks and I whisper a no.

"My great, I don't know how many greats, grandfather formed this pack. Back then there weren't many wolves and mates were quite rare. When one found there mate, they were treasured so much because they are sacred and gifts from the goddess. My grandfather did not think he would get a mate so he didn't even bother looking, until he found her. He was mesmerized and completely enchanted by her.

She loved stars and the moon and each and every night, my grandfather-- let's call him that, would find her staring at the sky, at the moon and the stars. So one time, he sat with her and asked her what she loved the most, and she said the stars. But the stars were so many, littered across the sky and the moon was at the centre, getting all the attention, surrounded and guarded. My grandfather pointed towards the moon and told her that he was the stars and she was his moon. Guarded protected, loved and completely enchanting, but because she loved the stars, he named the pack after the stars his soulmate loved watching." He relays and I'm almost in tears. It's such a beautiful story, one that is not told anymore.

Christian takes my hands in his, and my eyes meet his and for the first time I understand the emotions there, the emotions that has always been there but I had been too naive to realize and understand.

"You're my moon, Ciane and I'm the stars that surround you." He says and I'm crying. Who knew this once cold man would be this sweet, this genuine. I'm in utter shock.

"I love you," He continues and I sob. I have always seen it in his eyes and I yet I never understood it.

I throw my arms around his neck and we almost fall to the ground.

"I love you too, Christian." It wasn't a lie.

I can't believe it. I can't believe I actually found someone who loves me and I do them.

Our peace doesn't last long though.

"Aww, this is so beautiful!" Olivia screams almost bursting my sensitive ears.

I turn to glare at Olivia who is grinning like a mad woman. Jonah stands next to her, holding their one year old daughter, a small smile on his lips.

When the pack was disbanded, Jonah automatically decided he was never going to leave his mate again and would follow her wherever she went. Christian had made him his beta which he had totally not expected. Christian had never apologized for almost killing him when he found out Olivia was pregnant. It was quite obvious he's too overprotective over her, especially after what had happened.

"What are you doing here?" Christian grumbles when I detach myself from him.

"Can't I just visit my brother for no reason?" Olivia mocks and I walk over to her, pulling her in a hug.

"Don't listen to him, he's just acting like a child."

Jonah and Olivia had purchased a house not far from the pack house where I was staying. Jonah's parents also lived quite close to their home and would often babysit Alicia.

"I saw that. I need details. Not too much though." Olivia whispers in my ear and I blush.

I stare at Jonah who gives me a grin and I return it.

"Let me have her." I say as I take Alicia from him. Such a cutie she is.

I never expected, not even in my wildest imagination, that I'd be happy after what Exus did. After the things he almost destroyed in me. Over time, I had decided to move forward and doing so was by forgetting the pain he had caused me, not the lesson learnt. For me to move forward, I had to remove him from my heart and my mind, the need to get back at him. And I did. I was happy, very and I couldn't ask for anything more. This was everything I've ever dreamed of.